GALLERY BUNDU

Also by Paul Stoller

Black American English (editor)
In Sorcery's Shadow (with Cheryl Olkes)
Fusion of the Worlds
The Taste of Ethnographic Things
The Cinematic Griot: The Ethnography of Jean Rouch
Embodying Colonial Memories
Sensuous Scholarship
Jaguar
Money Has No Smell
Stranger in the Village of the Sick

To J-P + Elli
my dear, dear friends
with love,
Paul
05.26.05

GALLERY BUNDU

A Story about an African Past

Paul Stoller

THE UNIVERSITY OF CHICAGO PRESS
CHICAGO AND LONDON

PAUL STOLLER teaches anthropology at West Chester University and Temple University. He is the author of numerous books, including *Money Has No Smell* and *Jaguar,* both published by the University of Chicago Press.

The University of Chicago Press, Chicago 60637
The University of Chicago Press, Ltd., London
© 2005 by The University of Chicago
All rights reserved. Published 2005
Printed in the United States of America

14 13 12 11 10 09 08 07 06 05   1 2 3 4 5

ISBN: 0-226-77523-2 (cloth)
ISBN: 0-226-77524-0 (paper)

LIBRARY OF CONGRESS CATALOGING-IN-PUBLICATION DATA

Stoller, Paul.
    Gallery Bundu : a story about an African past / Paul Stoller.
        p. cm.
    ISBN 0-226-77523-2 (cloth : alk. paper) — ISBN 0-226-77524-0
(pbk. : alk. paper)
    1. Art—Fiction.   2. Memory—Fiction.   3. Africa—Fiction.
I. Title.
    PS3569.T62277G35 2005
    813'.54—dc22

                                                    2004025708

⊗ The paper used in this publication meets the minimum requirements of the American National Standard for Information Sciences—Permanence of Paper for Printed Library Materials, ANSI Z39.48-1992.

For Jasmin

Bundu:

1. a log
2. a wooden post
3. wood
4. (African) art

Songhay-English dictionary

Stories are for joining the past to the future. Stories are for those late hours in the night when you can't remember how you got from where you were to where you are. Stories are for eternity, when memory is erased, when there is nothing to remember except the story.

Tim O'Brien, *The Things They Carried*

NIGER 1971

I'm one of those unfortunate souls who live too much in the past. Don't get me wrong; I like my life in the present. I co-own a gallery of African art in New York City and I live and work with Elli Farouch, who is beautiful and vivacious—the love of my life. As they say in West Africa, our life together is sweet. Sometimes, though, Elli finds it difficult to tolerate my peculiarities. That's understandable. It's not easy, after all, to live in the present with someone who spends too much time in the past. My dilemma is that I can't seem to stop thinking about a whole series of past events that have twisted and turned me in unimaginable directions. These memories, to steal from Wordsworth, are too much with me.

Nearly thirty years ago, when I lived in far away West Africa, I was a young, brash, secondary schoolteacher. Way back then, I actually thought I could control my destiny. Those feelings of total self-control began to change on a blisteringly hot day in June 1971.

I remember that day as if it were yesterday. I was sitting behind a battered aluminum desk in a sweltering classroom, trying to grade a particularly bad set of exams. The heat had given me a dull headache and sweat had soaked my shirt, which stuck to my back in wet patches. A squadron of three flies buzzed around my head. That was a scene far from paradise. Three fateful claps broke the sweaty stillness of the afternoon. A roomful of eyes focused on a young boy standing at the threshold of my classroom. He wore a dirty pair of khaki shorts and a torn T-shirt.

"Yes?" I asked. "What is it?"

"A telegram for Monsieur Lyons," the boy responded in a shaky voice.

My stomach tightened. Like most people, I associated telegrams with bad news. For almost a year I had been teaching English in Tillaberi, a small town in Niger, one of the hottest countries of the world. In two weeks I would complete the second half of my two-year Peace Corps tour and return to America. I hoped the telegram wasn't going to spoil my homecoming. "Where's it from?"

"It's from Niamey."

I took a deep breath of relief. No bad news from the United States, I told myself. It was probably a missive from the Peace Corps office, which was located in the capital city.

The boy handed me the telegram, which was from Zeinabou, my girlfriend.

DAVID LYONS. COME AS SOON AS POSSIBLE.
WE HAVE TO TALK. ZEINABOU

My anxiety immediately returned. Why had Zeinabou sent a note of such urgency? I had been seeing her, off and on, for more than a year. Tall and lithe with a luminous heart-shaped face, she was the most beautiful woman I had ever known. What could she need that warranted a telegram? When could I leave? It was Thursday afternoon. Because Friday was a light teaching day, I could get away in midmorning and with luck be in Niamey by noon. That would give me the weekend with Zeinabou. I sent her a telegram, telling her I'd see her in Niamey on Friday afternoon.

The next morning the bus made an unusually speedy trip to Niamey. I disembarked at the bus station, took a taxi to the water tower that marked Nouveau Marché, a neighborhood of functionaries and merchants just south of Niamey's central district, and walked down a dusty, rutted side street to Zeinabou's home. She lived in a three-room mudbrick house squeezed into a rectangular compound with five similar dwellings, all hidden from the street by an eight-foot mud-brick wall.

Zeinabou came to the door in an indigo blue top with a matching wraparound. She kissed me on each cheek and let me in. Like the proper hostess, she had prepared tea. "Sit down," she said softly.

Her composure intensified my anxiety. Afraid of what she might say, I ran my fingers through my hair.

"I'm pregnant," she said breaking an unusually uncomfortable silence between us, "and you're the father."

Oh shit, I said to myself. My eyes began to twitch and I scratched my shoulder. How could this happen? I had had two great years in Niger, but now I wanted to move on. I truly cared for Zeinabou, but I had plans for graduate school, for a life in America. I didn't want a more permanent relationship with her. Besides, we had never talked of marriage. I had been very careful with Nigerien women, including Zeinabou. Realizing that I had apparently come to what people in Niger called a point of misfortune, I took a deep breath. I was a twenty-four-year-old about to make a decision that could shape the rest of my life. "Are you sure?" I asked her, unable to think of anything else to say.

Zeinabou stiffened. "Of course I'm sure. I've been pregnant before," she said tersely.

"Have you been tested?"

"No," she said firmly. She sipped her tea. "The baby is yours. Do you doubt that?"

I stretched my arms and cracked my knuckles. Zeinabou had occasionally slept with other men. "I'm not sure, Zeinabou." My heart raced. I paused a moment and sighed. "I'm sorry."

Zeinabou leaned forward. "I'm going to have this baby. I want to know what you are going to do about it."

"I don't know," I admitted. "I've got to think."

"I thought you were different, but maybe you're just like the others," she said harshly. "You want your pleasure, but refuse to be a man when you need to be. You make us pregnant, return home, and leave behind your own flesh and blood." Zeinabou leaned toward me and put her hands on her knees. "Are you willing to take care of me and your child?"

Needing time to think and ponder my responsibilities, I didn't know how to answer. "I don't know what to do."

"I think I already know what you're going to do," Zeinabou scoffed. "If you decide to behave like a man, you know where to find me." She looked away. "Please leave now."

There was nothing that I could add. Ashamed of myself, I stood up and left. Two weeks later I sent Zeinabou all of my extra money with a goodbye note and returned to America with a troubled heart.

NEW YORK 1998

That fateful day seems like yesterday. Elli tells me I think about it too much. When I dream about it, I wake up with heart palpitations. What would have happened if I had said yes to Zeinabou? Alas, I did not say yes. I'm in New York City working at Gallery Bundu rather than in Niamey. Elli has been helping me to confront the past. Progress has been slow, but several days ago I took a small step toward psychological closure.

I was sitting comfortably behind Gallery Bundu's narrow counter, drinking tea with Elli. She is a tall, dark Lebanese woman in her late thirties. Her presence blends well with the West African statuary she has spotlighted on shelves and pedestals—slender and shadowy figures in the dim light. As on most days, she was dressed casually in black—a round-necked cashmere sweater offset by a simple silver rope necklace and a long wool skirt that partially covered black boots. Her long black hair, parted in the middle, frames an elegant oval face marked by lustrous olive skin, an aristocratically thin nose, a narrow, sensuous mouth, and large hazel eyes. I met Elli in 1991 at the American Embassy in Niger, where she worked as a clinical psychologist. We fell in love and have been together ever since. On the day in question, we had been suffering through a slow business cycle, and Elli was hoping that the new shipment of objects we were expecting might spark some new sales.

I'm a tall man of 52 years. My hair is still long, thick, and black. Call me vain, but I'm proud that I don't use hair dye. My beard is also black, but laced with streaks of white. I have a broad nose and prominent cheekbones—strong features. Elli says that my face is softened by a thin mouth and deep-set brown eyes.

That morning, as on most mornings, Elli sipped her tea and listened to classical music. Tea and music would ground her for the day. I've always preferred the blues, but Elli has never allowed me to play blues in the gallery. Blues and African art are like oil and water, Elli always says—bad for business.

"I'm nervous about this shipment," Elli announced. "I hope Mamadou Demba brings us good pieces today. How long has he been away?"

"Five months."

"Five months," she repeated. "Maybe he brought back some real finds?"

"I hope so." During the first three years of Gallery Bundu, which translates to "gallery of wood," I spent much of my spare time traveling through West Africa with my partner, Diop, in search of fine sculpture and masks. The expense and strain of travel, however, soon became a burden on the business. In time we found it more economical to receive shipments from Diop or to look for African art in New York City, where West African traders have established The Warehouse, a huge repository in Chelsea.

When I left the pregnant Zeinabou in Niger, I returned home to study art history. But I also wanted to study with Amadu, a master weaver among the Songhay people. So after graduate school at Yale, I returned to Niger and spent one year with Amadu. Besides explaining to me the techniques and symbolism of West African weaving, he taught me what it meant to "weave the world." I graduated from Yale and then joined the Art History Department at Bendix College, in Bernardsville, New Jersey. I've been teaching there for twenty years. Students usually like my courses. Colleagues have spoken positively about my published work. As for my business skills, they are, to be honest, very much lacking. Thank God Elli, who comes from a family of Lebanese merchants, has always insisted that I refrain from discussing prices with the art traders.

Elli looked down at her teacup. "I hope they can unload in front of the store."

"So do I."

Looking out the storefront window, she suddenly jumped up. "You better go out there and stand in that empty parking space that just opened up. Go now. Grab your coat and be sure to stand your ground," she ordered quickly, as she shoved me out the door before I could object.

I soon found myself out in the cool, penetratingly moist November air, guarding an open parking spot on Spring Street in Soho. I waited and watched, and after almost twenty minutes in the damp chill, I wondered when the traders were going to show. I was looking for a van. Standing in an open parking spot, as you might imagine, is a dangerous pursuit in Manhattan. Two people seeking the precious parking spot had already cursed me.

"Who do you think you are?" complained a heavyset man in a delivery truck. "You can't just stand there."

Another man, in a red Pontiac Grand Am, tried to nudge me away by actually inching his car into the space. Wrapped in my ample down jacket and anchored by bulky hiking boots, I somehow managed to stand firm.

"Are you crazy? You gonna get yourself killed out here." Giving up, the man drove away.

When was Mamadou going to arrive? I stewed. Why do these Africans always have to be late? Gritty gallery work had become increasingly irritating. I love to collect African art, but can't stand selling it. I enjoy wonderful conversations with traders on buying trips in Africa, but hate the tedious details of mounting an exhibit in New York. I feel comforted by the presence of ancestral statues and spirit masks, but my collection of "wood," the term African traders use to describe their art, also makes me sad. It's another reminder of the past—of Zeinabou and all that I've lost.

The sound of Mamadou's sputtering white Econoline van jolted me back to the present. I waved vigorously and the van crept toward the parking spot on the street. I breathed a sigh of relief.

THREE

Mamadou Demba is a tall, barrel-chested man who takes pride in his sense of style. He wore black dress slacks, a brown silk shirt, and a new-looking leather jacket. He smiled as he stepped onto the sidewalk, exposing a perfect set of gleaming white teeth.

"David, I am happy to see you," he said pleasantly. We had met the previous year at The Warehouse.

"I am also happy to see you," I said, "but I almost got killed protecting this parking space."

Mamadou stared at me quizzically. "America," he stated, "is a very strange place. Very strange."

Another man stepped onto the street from the passenger side. His short, slight frame was draped by a black down jacket frayed at the cuffs and a shabby pair of khaki trousers. He wore a New York Yankees baseball cap and oil-stained hiking boots. He walked toward Mamadou and me.

"This is Daouda Kouyate, my helper," Mamadou said, pointing toward his colleague. "It's his first time in America and he speaks no English."

I shook the helper's hand and greeted him in French. As is the custom in West Africa, we inquired after each other's families. Years before I had learned that it was impolite to jump right into business matters.

Mamadou looked back at the van. "I'm hoping we can do some business today." He strolled to the van's back door and opened it, revealing a space in which every square inch was stuffed with African art. "We have a fine shipment of wood here," he said. "Tell Elli we brought you good things this time—with good prices. We'll be ready to talk in a little while."

I walked back into the gallery and flashed Elli a sarcastic smile. "They almost killed me out there."

"I noticed," she said, looking at the gallery's books. "How long before they're ready with their display?"

"Who knows?" I was a bit irritated at her lack of sympathy. "They said they'd be a little while."

"I'll need your help on this, David," she said, trying to appease me. She's always trying to appease me, a charitable way to adapt to my "issues." "I don't want you to bargain, but can you tell me what's really good?"

"Okay," I agreed with some relief. "Besides, you always bargain for the best deal."

Elli is an excellent bargainer; it's a skill she acquired as a child surrounded by merchants in Lebanon. She stared out the storefront window at the Africans. They were unloading their cargo, which they arranged in rows on the sidewalk. A small crowd of onlookers had stopped to observe the proceedings.

"I better go out and greet them. Don't want to be rude," she said. She slipped on a short black leather jacket, walked outside, and shook Mamadou's giant, fleshy hand.

"Ah, Elli. It has been so long since we last met."

"Far too long, Mamadou. How are your wife and your children?" They exchanged pleasantries for a few moments before Mamadou asked after the business.

"We get by with God's help," Elli intoned, following traditional West African as well as Middle Eastern salutatory traditions.

"May God be with us all," Mamadou answered. He looked at his helper, who continued to unload art objects. "Please excuse me, Elli, but I must return to work. We'll be ready to talk business soon."

Elli came back into the shop. Twenty minutes later we walked out to a sidewalk that had been transformed into an African art bazaar. Dozens of objects were on display: statues, stools, chairs, masks, textiles, and beads. Closest to the curb, Mamadou had arranged a line of ten Ashanti stools, three-foot rectangular structures from Ghana. Their curved seats make them look like miniature pagodas. Next to the Ashanti stools were Dogon stools from Mali, which take the form of flat-backed donkeys—four hooves, a neck, a head, and a tail. There was a low wooden bed, perhaps seven feet long, supported by four substantial pegs.

"These are stunning pieces," I said.

Elli's eye focused on a pair of short figures, one male and one female, into whose long-necked bodies the artist had carved swirling patterns. At the center of the display stood a three-foot pile of antique kente, brightly colored geometric patterns of silk cloth cut into strips that had been sewn together to create regal togas. As Elli caressed the cloth, I looked at Mamadou. Holding his hands behind his back, he stood stiffly, rocking back and forth on his heels. His face beamed with pride.

"How do you like the presentation?" he asked.

"It's impressive," said Elli.

"Very creative," I said.

Mamadou had unpacked five majestically tall male ancestor figures from Congo. One of the pieces had a masked face decorated with brass tacks. The figures had ample potbellies, and except for one, had had their penises cut off.

"I think that's to excise their power before they're sold," I explained to Elli.

Mamadou strolled over to them, ready to talk business. "You can buy the whole display . . . only $20,000."

Because I'm excluded from bargaining, I politely excused myself. "I'll go inside and make lunch." Mamadou and I shook hands. "After you're finished you must come in and sample my African cooking."

"With pleasure," Mamadou said.

Elli knows that the bargaining process between gallery owner and West African trader is a complex one. Once the presentation is made, the trader almost always suggests that you buy the entire collection. Maybe the trader needs quick money to pay off debts to one of his associates. Maybe he wants to liquidate his inventory and return quickly to West Africa. Like most gallery owners, Elli always turns down these "generous" offers. Sometimes she counters the offer by asking if any of the pieces have "papers," records of where and when the art was first collected and by whom, a lineage of subsequent owners, and a list of the places and dates of their exhibition showings.

Elli was sure that Mamadou's pieces had no provenance, but, true to form, she asked him anyway to secure a bargaining advantage—albeit a fleeting one.

Laughter rippled through Mamadou's body. "How long have you been doing business," he asked, "three, four years? You should know better than to ask such a question."

"Well??? . . . I'll ask it all the same."

"As you know, dear lady, if you want papers, I can find some for you," he said, referring to the fact that provenance can be as easily fabricated as art can be reproduced.

"That's okay, Mamadou." She took a good look at the display. "Let me get my clipboard and we'll get down to business."

Clipboard in hand, Elli returned to the "presentation."

"How much for the Ashanti stool at the end?" she asked.

"You don't like the other ones?" Mamadou wondered.

"These are good pieces, Mamadou," she said, "but I have to think of my market. How much?"

Mamadou walked over to the stool in question and picked it up. The patina of its curved seat glimmered in the dull morning light. "For you, Elli, $150."

Elli stared at him and smiled. "I'll give you $75. Shall I write it down?" she asked. Once a price has been noted, it is firm.

Mamadou laughed. "Have you been to Africa lately?" he queried, complimenting her bargaining skill.

"No, but my Lebanese ancestors were great traders themselves."

"Okay, $100 for that piece."

"Good. Have your helper set it aside."

It was a tedious process. Every piece that interested Elli had to be discussed and compared to other like pieces. The discussions had to be diplomatic in order to maintain respect for Mamadou's reputation as a trader of first-rate African art. Sometimes Elli went on about her particular tastes or about what was driving prices up or down in New York—all to convince him of her seriousness as well as to demonstrate her respect for his considerable knowledge.

An hour later, Elli looked over her clipboard. She had agreed to buy twenty-five pieces. As always, she feared that she was paying too much for some of the objects but was pleased that she had gotten good buys on others. She waved Mamadou over to where she was standing. "We've noted twenty-five objects and the total comes to $5,250. Shall we go through it again with my calculator?"

Mamadou patted her hand and commented, "What is business without trust? . . . It is nothing without trust," he added, answering his own question. "Dear Elli, go and write me a check."

He asked his helper to carry the purchased pieces into the gallery. As the men entered, I looked admiringly at the African trader. Mamadou had a deep knowledge of African art. Many people in the art world would look at a man like Mamadou and consider him nothing more than an ignorant "runner," a seller of commodities. I once thought the same way. But my years at Gallery Bundu had reinforced my profound respect for men like Mamadou, men who, with great care, shepherd art from Africa to America. "You brought some beautiful pieces today," I said to him.

"Thank you, David. May the pieces sell well—and quickly," Mamadou said, as Elli handed him a check. "As always, it is a pleasure to do business with you two."

"Please join us for lunch," Elli said, reaffirming my previous invitation. She looked at me and smiled. "He's made one of his African sauces."

"Beef in bitter leaf sauce," I acknowledged proudly.

"That's one of my favorites." Mamadou said something in his language to Daouda, who responded by vigorously nodding his head. "We're delighted. You two have become real Africans."

We sat down on four wooden stools arranged around a low table. In the traditional African style, I served lunch in a large gourd filled with rice and a smaller bowl of steaming sauce. I also brought in two bowls filled with water—a small one for drinking and a larger one for hand washing.

"Ah," said Mamadou, seeing the two bowls. "This will be a real African meal. Praise be to God."

I dipped my right hand into the larger bowl and recited a brief incantation in Songhay giving thanks for nature's bounty. I then rolled a small ball of rice in my hand and dipped it into the sauce. The others followed suit.

We ate in silence, because in Africa eating is considered very serious business—not to be interrupted with conversation.

When everyone had finished, I passed the water bowl. Mamadou took a big drink and passed it on to his compatriot. "David," he said, "that was very good sauce. I have proof now that you lived in Africa. But how did you learn to cook African food so well?" he asked. He looked at me for several moments. "You must have had an African wife."

I looked down, flustered. I didn't really want to talk about Zeinabou—it was much too painful. Keeping the pain pretty much to myself, I had revealed the details of my past life in Africa only to a small number of close friends. But Elli, ever the psychologist, had patiently encouraged me to talk about my past. She had even suggested that I write a book about my life. "No," I said, "I learned by watching a woman prepare dinner." I paused. Should I go on? I looked at Elli and took the plunge. "She was my girlfriend," I said uneasily.

"Same thing as a wife," Mamadou declared.

"Africa is always in my thoughts," I said, avoiding a direct response to Mamadou's declaration. "I learned a great deal there."

"I'd like to hear more," Mamadou insisted. Sensing that I had much to tell, he looked into my eyes.

"It's a long story," I said with hesitation. Maybe it would be therapeutic to recount my story to Mamadou? Here was a man that I liked and admired.

Like many Africans, Mamadou loved to listen to stories and rarely passed up an opportunity to hear a good one. He leaned forward on his stool. "I'd love to hear it, my friend. If you know Africa, you know that we always make time to hear good stories."

WEST AFRICA 1969–71

FOUR

My first experience in Africa occurred in September 1969 when an
Air Afrique jet landed in Freetown, Sierra Leone, en route to Abi-
djan, Côte d'Ivoire. The all-night flight, which had originated in
Paris, touched down at six thirty. For security reasons, the passengers,
all of whom were Peace Corps volunteers bound for Francophone
West Africa, had to remain onboard. The captain cut the engine and
turned off the air-conditioning. Flight attendants opened the jet's
forward and rear doors, allowing air—African air—to stream in.
Never in my twenty-two years had I been assailed by such humidity.
All the passengers immediately began to perspire.

"How long do we have to stay in the plane?" I asked one of the
flight attendants.

"One hour, maybe longer," she responded. "The transit lounge is
air-conditioned, but they won't allow you in there."

"Why not?" another passenger asked.

"New regulations, I think."

"Could I get some water?" I asked. She looked at me with some
sympathy. At the time my face was thin and framed by a thick, poorly
trimmed beard and wavy, shoulder-length black hair.

"Sorry, but we're out of water. In a little while they should bring
some from the airport, along with breakfast."

After a sweaty hour, the planeload of Peace Corps volunteers began to complain about the uncomfortable conditions. I had joined
the Peace Corps for multiple reasons, the major one being a deferment from the draft. In 1969, you see, Peace Corps service qualified as
an occupational deferment—a way to avoid going to Vietnam. Ser-

vice in the Peace Corps was much less painful than draft resistance or flight to Canada. What's more, many of the draft-dodging male volunteers simply wanted to have an adventure and a good time in Africa: get high or drunk—or both—and, of course, sleep with as many women as possible. Now they faced their first less-than-romantic encounter with Africa.

"We fly all night without food," one young man headed for Togo grumbled, "and now we have to sit in this damn plane for no apparent reason. I wish I had a beer."

Others agreed. Several attendants, dressed in starched white uniforms with epaulets, walked toward the plane. Food and water were finally on the way. The first group brought breakfast—boxes with a croissant, butter, and yogurt. Other attendants followed with water, coffee, and tea. My body ached from fatigue and hunger. When I received my box breakfast, I hungrily consumed the yogurt and then savored a strong and flavorful cup of coffee.

I was beginning to enjoy my first meal on African soil. When I broke the croissant in two, however, I discovered that a large, thick green bug had been baked into the roll.

The guy sitting next to me, Stevie Hunter, who was going to spend his two-year tour in Côte d'Ivoire, looked over my shoulder and laughed. He slapped me on the back. "Welcome to Africa, David," he said. "Welcome to Africa."

FIVE

Two days later I found myself seated in a sidewalk café in Abidjan's exclusive Plateau neighborhood. I had ventured out with Stevie and Frank Pascone, who, like me, was headed for Niger, to escape the boredom of the Peace Corps orientation for a few hours. Hungry for a decent meal, we wanted to sample the gourmet food in the Plateau quarter, the Abidjan neighborhood with a decidedly French flavor.

The Peace Corps had installed us in the Grand Hotel, a shuttered colonial-style dwelling built around a tropical courtyard. In the center of the courtyard was a slimy pool filled with baby crocodiles. Each day we had to go to Peace Corps headquarters for orientation sessions. Most of the meetings had been eminently forgettable, the one exception being the session on health in Africa, for which men and women had been separated.

"We are going to be frank," said the Peace Corps director, who led the men's discussion. "There are many snakes in Africa. Rule of thumb: if you make a lot of noise, the green mambas won't bother you. We mention snakes to acquaint you with your Peace Corps medical kit. Each one of you will receive a kit that contains hypodermic needles and two kinds of antivenom: one for mambas and one for vipers. We expect you to use the hypodermic needles only to treat snakebite." The director snickered. "We have had reports that some volunteers have been distilling the opium in their paregoric, which is also in your kit, and then mainlining it with the hypodermic needles."

"Wow," someone in the crowd said admiringly, "that's far out."

"We trust you not to do that," the director emphasized. "And one other thing, gentleman," he continued. "As you know, there are many beautiful women in Africa. You can go right across the bridge near your hotel and walk to Treichville and find prostitutes in any bar."

"We should go tomorrow night," Stevie suggested to me.

"We won't tell you not to see prostitutes or other women. It is inevitable that you will want to be sexually active during your two years here. That is why we supply you with condoms. Venereal disease is very widespread here. So, gentlemen, please use the condoms. It's imperative."

This speech resulted in much excited discussion among the men.

"Gentlemen, gentlemen," the director said, trying to quiet the group. "You're about to embark on a great adventure. Be careful. Stay healthy. Welcome to Africa. It's an exciting place."

Thinking of the phrase "Welcome to Africa" brought me back to my present circumstances. I looked up to see our waiter, who, like the airport attendants in Sierra Leone, wore a starched white uniform with epaulets. The thin, broad-nosed man brought me a very European dish—*soupe à l'onion* topped with a thick layer of Gruyère cheese. Before coming to Africa, I had wanted to become a journalist and live in Chicago or New York City. Thoughts of Africa had never crossed my mind in those days. Circumstances, most of which are beyond our control, can sometimes transform our lives. Given my age and my fear of going to Vietnam, I now found myself, occupational deferment in hand, in steamy Abidjan, Côte d'Ivoire, eating *soupe à l'onion* at a sidewalk café.

My new friend, Frank, was short, thin, and dark with long black hair. Stevie, whom I had met on the plane, was tall and muscular with long blond hair, blue eyes, and a square chin. Stevie had a light-hearted approach to life that I admired but was not able to sustain, myself.

As we talked about the heat, the various diseases we needed to avoid, and the potential for sexual adventures, I heard a scraping sound. In the distance I saw a young man, wearing knee pads, crawling toward us. Dressed in a tattered T-shirt and a pair of filthy khaki shorts, the man proceeded with determination, his face frozen in a grimace.

We stopped eating. I put my hand on the low barrier that separated the sidewalk from the line of restaurant tables. The man crawled next to our table, grabbed the barrier and pulled himself off the pavement. He smiled at us warmly, revealing a mouthful of missing teeth.

"Good afternoon, gentlemen," he said in the very proper and formal French of educated Africans. "Because I can't walk, I can't work. I have to crawl everywhere in this city, which, as you can imagine, is very difficult. I have no money and I haven't eaten in two days. Would you kindly spare me a few francs? My hunger hurts me very much."

Although my French was not yet good, I quickly grasped the man's message. "We should give him something," I said. "He looks destitute."

"His take today will probably exceed our monthly allowance," Stevie said as I fumbled in my pocket.

"Don't be so cynical," Frank said to Stevie. "I'll give him some money, too." Frank gave me his contribution. Stevie shrugged and did the same. I handed the money over.

The man's smile broadened as he took the money. "May God bless you," he said, and he stood up and walked away.

Surprised at first, we laughed at ourselves. We had just observed another example of the complexity of our new life.

SIX

The next night Stevie, Frank, and I, together again after a long day of Peace Corps orientation, followed the Peace Corps director's directions to the good life in Abidjan. We crossed the bridge near our hotel and entered the world of Treichville, Abidjan's most populous neighborhood. Beneath us, a murky lagoon reflected dim street light. The heavy night air pressed against my shoulders. I felt excited but nervous walking into Treichville. I didn't know what to expect from the mysterious African night. Since my excitement exceeded my apprehension, I eagerly followed the seemingly fearless Stevie.

In Treichville the smell of human excrement permeated the air near the lagoon's shore, which functioned as a public toilet. We walked along what seemed to be Treichville's main boulevard, a four-lane roadway lined with buildings that resembled warehouses. Ten-foot cement walls, whose malodor indicated that the locals used them as convenient urinals, shielded the warehouses from the street. Farther on, small groups of people were sitting on the sidewalk. The murmur of street conversations reached us from some distance away. On the opposite sidewalk, a mother and a child slept on flattened cardboard boxes.

"Good evening, Toubab," a man said in French as we walked by. "Give us a gift," begged some children who ran up to us, their hands outstretched. "Toubab, Toubab, Toubab."

"*Toubab* means white man," the all-knowing Stevie informed us.

Minutes later Stevie pointed ahead to a brightly lit section of town. We heard highlife music in the distance.

"There are so many bars there!" Frank commented. "Which one should we go to?"

The area was like a neon canyon with many caves: Kit Kat Bar, Sign of Zorro Bar, Song of Roland Bar, Bar California, OK Bar, Hi Fi Bar, Soleil de Minuit (Midnight Sun) Bar, Dick Tracy Bar, Midi Bar. Young women dressed in short skirts and tight-fitting tops strolled along the sidewalks. A few of them said hello.

Stevie led us toward the Sign of Zorro Bar. "A man at the hotel recommended this one."

We entered a narrow, dimly lit space. The wooden bar stretched along one mirrored wall not far from the door. Large mirrors covered the bar's other walls. Nine or ten round tables had been arranged in the back, leaving a space for dancing toward the front of the bar. As we walked toward the tables, our shoes clacked on the gleaming hardwood floors. At the early hour of nine o'clock, we were the only customers. I noticed an old jukebox in the back corner. The rhythms of James Brown's "Papa's Got a Brand New Bag" filled the air.

As soon as we sat down and ordered beer, a group of scantily clad young women stampeded toward us. In total shock, I suddenly found a woman sitting on each of my thighs.

The woman on my left said: "Good evening, love. You are very young and beautiful. You come with me to see my room. I make you happy." She was short and plump and wore a wig, a red satin miniskirt, red stockings, a white tank top, and a big smile.

The woman on my right said: "No, love, come with me to my room. We go and in fifteen minutes you'll be happy. I know what toubabs like." She kissed my ear. Her red satin hot pants, black lace stockings, and black cotton top stretched taut over her tall, thin body. She ran her fingers through my thick hair. "So handsome. Come with me."

I looked across at Stevie, who also had two women on his lap. "Should we buy them drinks?" he suggested.

I ordered beers for everyone. Stevie quickly made arrangements to leave the bar with one of the women. After drinking one beer, he stood up. "See you back at the hotel, guys. Have fun," he said, walking out with a tall, shapely woman.

I looked somewhat anxiously over to Frank. "Do you really want to have sex with these women?" I asked. I had never had sex with a prostitute.

"Not really," said Frank. "Besides, I didn't bring protection. Did you?"

"No. I didn't expect such a big reception," I admitted.

"Why don't we finish our beers, excuse ourselves, and go back to the hotel," Frank added with some relief.

Excusing ourselves proved to be more difficult than we thought. The women held on to us. When I tried to stand up to go, my new friends tried to hold me down. Across the table, two women fought over Frank.

"Please," I pleaded in my inadequate French. "You are all very nice, but we need to go. Perhaps we'll come back another night."

The women talked animatedly in an African language. They pointed at Frank and me and laughed. Just then, three men, probably French, came through the door. The women left us as quickly as they had arrived and made their way toward the new customers.

We departed quickly and headed back to the hotel, our first sexual adventure in Africa having come to an unsatisfying end.

SEVEN

The following week I found myself in Bouaké, Côte d'Ivoire, a large town three hundred kilometers north of Abidjan. Bouaké, the second-largest city in the country, was situated at the border of the West African rain forest and the woodland savanna. It was also the central town of the Baulé people, one of whom, Houphoute Boigny, had been Côte d'Ivoire's president since independence in 1960.

I found the Baulé culture fascinating; it was more like the "real" Africa. I wanted to learn as much as I could about it. Every night during my first week in Bouaké, where the Peace Corps wanted us to learn how to teach English as a foreign language, I'd talk with Gregoire, my African mentor and an English teacher at a Bouaké secondary school. Gregoire was short and thin and had a smooth, round face that looked liked waxed ebony. One night Gregoire told me about the Baulé conception of the otherworld. Every person among the Baulé, Gregoire said, had a lover in the otherworld. People routinely dreamed about their otherworld lovers, and if the otherworld lovers felt slighted, they would disrupt the lives of their real-world counterparts. To avert these disasters, people would describe the characteristics of their otherworld lovers to a carver, who then fashioned a statuette in the lover's likeness. To protect themselves from angry otherworld lovers, people made regular offerings of food to the statuette and slept with it once a week. These acts kept the otherworld lovers happy.

The Baulé, Gregoire also told me, had sacred forests that were restricted to men who had been initiated into a secret society. If an uninitiated man or woman entered the forest, otherworld spirits would attack him or her.

"What happens if you get attacked?" I asked.

"Many bad things can happen," said Gregoire. "Last year, there was an American who was teaching in a small Baulé village. He was arrogant. He boasted that he didn't believe in spirits and that he could walk through any forest without ill effect. One afternoon he found the village's sacred forest and walked through it. That evening he developed a high fever and lost consciousness. The villagers rushed him to the hospital in Bouaké. The doctors evacuated him to Abidjan. They revived him, but his legs remained paralyzed. The Peace Corps sent him back to America. Eventually he learned to walk again, but only with crutches."

"Did you see this man?" I asked with no small measure of skepticism. How could a walk in a forest bring on paralysis? Even so, the story provoked interest as well as apprehension.

"Of course, I did," said Gregoire. "He is one of your trainers, John Lawton."

Jesus, I said to myself. John was a frail-looking man with wavy blond hair and a scraggly beard who used crutches to move around.

"All that happened to John, but he won't talk about it." Gregoire hesitated a brief moment. "It would be dangerous for him."

"Dangerous?" I asked.

Gregoire smiled. "This is Africa. Maybe you will learn something about us."

The Peace Corps housed us in the dormitory of the secondary school, located on the outskirts of town. The facilities resembled military barracks: lumpy single beds, creaky wooden floors, dull overhead lights, enforced curfews, and a smelly latrine on each floor. At night the air hung heavy and hot in the dorm. Worse yet, the netting designed to protect us from the malarial bites of voracious mosquitoes made the close quarters even stuffier. The staff thought these conditions would toughen us for our tours in the bush. Everybody complained about the conditions. After several sleepless nights, one of the men lost his temper.

"This is a damn shit pit," he shouted. "How can they put us up in this place? We can't sleep. The insects never shut up, and the mosquitoes are whining right next to my ear. The head smells like old shit."

"Hey," the ever-positive Stevie said, "at least the food is decent."

"You call that mush they serve . . . food?" the same voice protested. "That fufu is so thick, I've been constipated for days."

"Try drinking some palm wine," Stevie suggested. "It sure cleaned David out." The previous day I had drunk a large quantity of palm wine, which provoked violent gastrointestinal eruptions. "Make sure you get some that has been tapped late in the day—real strong stuff."

The next morning Stevie and I went to breakfast in the refectory on the first floor of the dorm. We sat by ourselves in a corner and ate doughy baguettes we had smeared with canned margarine, imported from Nigeria, and strawberry jam, imported from Hungary. We each sipped a large mug of Nescafé.

The training director, John Sauer, a tall, skinny man with a crew cut and freckled skin, stood up and loudly cleared his throat. Wire-rimmed glasses framed his thin face, and a tentlike red print shirt embossed with green palm trees hung loosely over his baggy khaki trousers. "Excuse me, folks," he said with ceremony, "but could I have your attention?" He paused a few moments. "Last night they killed three green mambas on the school grounds."

"Great news!" a chorus of voices proclaimed.

"Seriously," Sauer persisted. "They killed three mambas. Two were in the gardens surrounding the school's flagpole. The other one was in one of the outhouses."

"Gee Sauer," someone shouted, "having those mambas out there will build Peace Corps character."

"There are probably many more of them around," Sauer continued. "We've hired a snake hunter to kill them. I'm told he's very good. But please be careful. If you walk outside at night, carry a flashlight and make a lot of noise. The mambas don't like light or noise. At night, try to avoid the outhouses. Mamba venom works quickly."

This latest bit of news troubled me. I asked the apparently fearless Stevie if he was afraid.

"Not really," Stevie said. "I'm not going to let it worry me. After all, there's a snake hunter around."

"I'd like to meet the snake hunter," I admitted. I had never heard of such an occupation.

The next afternoon Francis, one of the Ivorian teachers, took me to a small grass hut at the edge of the school grounds.

"The snake hunter lives here," said Francis. "Maybe he's home."

"Does he speak French?" I asked.

"No, no. Like me, he speaks Senufo, the language of our people. We come from the north. Our people are famous for sculpture and magic—especially the magical powers of our hunters."

As Francis and I approached the hut, Francis clapped his hands three times. "It's the African way of knocking on the door," he informed me.

"Djéjé," he called. "Are you there?" Francis was a tall, slim man about twenty-five years old. He had a bony face covered by an uneven beard and wore a white shirt that contrasted sharply with his black face.

The wind shifted, and I suddenly felt a presence behind me. I turned around and saw a tall, burly man with a bush of black and white hair, standing motionless. He wore a coarse, homespun brown tunic over a pair of short white trousers that had been fashioned from thin Chinese cotton. Scores of little leather pouches had been sewn in rows onto the tunic. Curiously, my first instinct was to wonder how the homespun tunic had been woven. What purpose, I asked myself, did those strange leather pouches serve? The man stared at us. It was strange that I hadn't heard his approach. It was as if he had simply appeared.

Francis greeted the hunter pleasantly. They spoke rapidly in Senufo for several moments. Francis then translated for me.

"Djéjé says there are many snakes around this school and that he has killed six mambas in three days. There are also vipers."

"I don't think I need to know all the details," I said uneasily. Francis then explained my fear of snakes—especially the mamba—to the snake hunter.

The man's body shook with laughter. He asked Francis to ask me why toubabs were so afraid of snakes.

"I don't know," I admitted.

The snake hunter held out his hand. I shook it and was taken aback. Calluses and scars covered the outside of his hand, but the palm was surprisingly smooth and warm. It felt comforting. Through Francis, Djéjé explained that the men in his family had been hunters for as long as anyone could remember. His father had taught him how to track and trap game and how to find his way in the forests and grasslands. He had also taught him the great traditions of hunters—their stories, magic, and respect for nature. This knowledge was passed down from generation to generation. "It keeps us rooted to the earth and gives us great strength. We are not afraid," he said, smiling and nodding his head.

"The hunters," Francis continued, "have great traditions among our people—and many stories of the past. They also have a deep sense about people. They can grasp who you are in an instant. I think Djéjé likes you," he added.

The hunter then produced from his trouser pocket a small dark leather pouch shaped like a tiny eggplant. He held it out to me.

"Take this amulet and put it in your pocket. It will lighten your fear."

This unexpected act of kindness made me beam. Although I was skeptical about the amulet's power, I gladly accepted it and put it in my pocket.

The snake hunter said a few more words, which Francis translated. "He says to carry the amulet with you always. If you take good care of it, you will meet wise men."

Djéjé said goodbye and walked away, disappearing into a field of elephant grass that bordered the school grounds.

"You are very, very lucky," Francis said. "To have this amulet is very good."

Not wanting to offend Francis with my skepticism, I fingered the leather pouch in my pocket and agreed.

"See you at dinner," Francis said and left.

I looked out toward the field of elephant grass into which the hunter had disappeared. In the distance I saw a cluster of cottonwoods aglow in the late afternoon light. Just beyond the trees a series of green hills rolled toward the horizon. I wondered what it would be like to hunt with Djéjé. Could I, an urban kid from northeast Philadelphia, marshal the courage to traipse through the bush filled with snakes, scorpions, and occasional panthers? I had lived a life that had minimized personal risk. After my father died when I was ten years old, I became a timid boy. Growing up I tried to compensate for my lack of adventurousness by befriending more daring boys, people like Stevie Hunter, who led me toward excitement. I still followed this pattern. After all, I had followed Stevie Hunter to Treichville, only to refuse a

prostitute's sexual invitation. No protection, I told myself. I had em-
ployed this follow-the-leader tactic for more than twelve years now. It
hadn't diminished my fears. If only I had had a father to guide me as I
grew up! Unlike the Senufo hunters, my family had never been very
big on ceremony or tradition. My mother, in fact, had been a busy single parent who lost much of her enthusiasm for life when my father
died. How lucky it would have been, I thought, to be part of an age-
old tradition like that of the Senufo hunters—a tradition that helped
adherents master their fears and anxieties.

As the sun slipped below the horizon, deep red and orange clouds
streaked across the western sky like so many flames. A cool breeze
kicked up and brought with it the smell of wood smoke. In Niger, I
wanted to meet people like the Senufo hunter. If I did, I told myself,
I'd try to learn their language, their history, and their customs. As I
saw it, this brief exposure to the Senufo hunter was a sign for me to
familiarize myself with African traditions.

EIGHT

One week after my encounter with the Senufo snake hunter, I found
myself in much more agreeable surroundings. I was one of only four
new Peace Corps volunteer English teachers in Niger that year, and
the government wanted to demonstrate its appreciation. A government chauffeur met us on the tarmac of the airport. A tall, thick man
with a bulging neck, the chauffeur looked elegant as he walked toward our plane in a flowing white damask robe. I complimented him
on his appearance.

"I am pleased you like my grand boubou," the man said. "My
name is Hamidou, and I will clear you through the formalities and
take you to your villa."

In short order, Hamidou shepherded us through the airport, a
converted hangar. We found our luggage, cleared customs, and, with
Hamidou's help, loaded our gear into a large Land Rover. He drove us
through the darkness on one of the few paved roads in Niamey, the
capital city.

"You'll be staying at a government villa for the next two weeks," he informed us. "This is a great honor reserved for important people. After you leave, in fact, the next guest will be General Mobutu from Zaire."

"Why are we getting such special treatment?" Susan Brown, one of the other teachers, asked in impeccable French.

"We believe that teachers are important to the future of the country. President Diori was a teacher, and he has the greatest respect for you." Hamidou drove us onto a tree-lined road bordered by spacious villas and government buildings. He pointed out the majestic Presidential Palace, a whitewashed mansion with shuttered windows and wrought-iron balconies. Several moments later, he turned off the road and drove down a gravel driveway that circled a fountain. A man in a chef's hat and apron stood in the doorway of a massive two-story villa.

We got out of the Land Rover and admired our new accommodations.

The man in the chef's hat spoke to us. "My name is Abdou. I'll be your chef for one week." He beckoned us inside. We walked into a spacious living room with a black leather sofa and two overstuffed black leather chairs. The walls were adorned with blankets woven in strips of deep green, black, red, and yellow. The tiled floor was covered with an assortment of oriental carpets and one large lion-skin rug. Table lamps and a large chandelier illuminated the room.

While the chef's assistant hauled our luggage upstairs to the bedrooms, the chef asked us to follow him into the dining room, where the table had been set. "We have been waiting for you. Please sit down and allow me to serve you dinner. You must be hungry."

Dumbfounded by the contrast between life in Niger and that in Côte d'Ivoire, we sat down. The chef opened a bottle of white wine. "It's a very fine Muscadet de Sevres," he said as he poured us each a glass. Being a Muslim, he poured himself a glass of bottled water. Holding up his glass, he proposed a toast. "Welcome to Niger," he said, beaming. After we clinked our glasses, Abdou took a sip of his water and disappeared into the kitchen.

"What's going on? It's not supposed to be like this," said Susan, troubled by flashes of the good life in squalid Niger.

"I could get used to this," said Frank Pascone.

"So could I," I nodded.

George Martin, the fourth member of the group, sipped his wine and said nothing.

We were then served an exquisite meal: potato mushroom soup, grilled leg of lamb, carrot salad, and a bottle of Bordeaux. For dessert, Abdou had baked an assortment of pastries. When we had finished, the chef bade us good night. "You must be tired," he said. "I'll serve breakfast at seven in the morning. I understand you have to be at work tomorrow at eight o'clock."

"Excuse me, sir," Susan said, "but where did you learn to cook so well?"

Abdou smiled at them. "Five years ago," he said proudly, "the government sent me to Paris to learn at the Cordon Bleu School. Now I cook for official banquets and for guests of the government like you."

NINE

The two luxurious weeks at the villa passed all too quickly. In the mornings, I enthusiastically studied French and Songhay, the African language spoken in Tera, the town where I had been assigned. In the afternoons, after a sumptuous lunch and a siesta, we walked around Niamey. I tried to practice Songhay and French during these outings. I went to the National Museum and Zoo and toured the central market, where I bought a Songhay blanket typical of the Tera region. Mostly, Frank and I wandered the streets, talked to people, and sampled street-roasted mutton or what had quickly become my favorite, *chenchena*, fried bean cakes.

Time passed quickly, though, and before I could get used to the good life in Niamey, I received an official letter from the Ministry of Education, ordering me to report in two days' time to the bus depot, where I would take "le car" for Tera, an isolated Songhay town located in Niger's far-western corner. During the final two days at the villa, I bought supplies: a mosquito net, a gas burner, and canned food. A tailor made me an African-style suit, a "The Sahelian," which is a pair of khaki trousers and a matching loose-fitting short-sleeved cotton shirt with two breast pockets and epaulets.

As I said goodbye to the other teachers, I felt a mixture of sadness, anxiety, and excitement. During the two weeks at the villa I had enjoyed unimaginable luxury. What would I find in Tera? How would my colleagues and students respond to me? My excitement outweighed my concerns, however. Tera, in the heart of the Nigerien bush, promised to be the site of adventure. If I learned to speak the Songhay language well, I might get to know someone like the Senufo snake hunter.

Wanting to impress the headmaster in Tera, I put on my new Sahelian suit. At 7:45 in the morning, the chauffeur put my luggage in the Land Rover and drove me to the bus depot. "Tera's an interesting place," the chauffeur said. "It's far away and you have to cross the river to get there. There's a ferry about sixty kilometers north. The river is very beautiful up there."

"That's good," I said tentatively.

The driver stopped the Land Rover at the bottom of a hill. It was eight o'clock, the hour of my scheduled departure. "We're here," he announced.

"Is this the depot?" I asked, looking out onto a large rectangle of blacktop bordered by stalls of food and dry goods vendors. I could see several Peugeot *camionnettes*—little pickup trucks—and two buses.

The chauffeur waved in the direction of the buses. "One of those may be going to Tera," he said as he unloaded my things. "Someone will let you know which bus to get on." The chauffeur shook my hand. "It was a pleasure getting to know you, Monsieur David. May God protect you on your journey."

As I walked into the depot carrying my luggage, I took in the distant buses, noticing several youths seated inside, their arms dangling from open windows. A young boy pushed a wooden cart across the center of the blacktop. "Coca, Esprit, Youki. Coca, Esprit, Youki. Cold." To the left I saw a spindly old woman seated on a palm-frond mat. A shawl of black cotton cloth covered her head; she was dressed in a homespun indigo wraparound garment. Lost in thought, she spat out a wad of tobacco. "Excuse me, madam," I said in my best Songhay. "Which bus goes to Tera?"

"Tera?"

I nodded eagerly.

The woman pointed to the bus that had its hood open. "That one," she said.

I observed the bus more closely. A man had crawled underneath the engine. My ticket indicated that the bus would leave at 8:00 a.m. "When does the bus leave?" I asked.

"Who knows?" the woman shrugged, looking curiously at the white man who had addressed her in Songhay. "Maybe it will leave in a little while." She moved to one side of her mat and invited me to sit down. "Sit down and rest, young man. You need to prepare yourself for your trip."

What did that mean? I sat down beside her.

The woman offered me kola nuts, which many Africans chew as a stimulant.

"Thank you, but I don't chew."

"You'll need something to strengthen you for the trip." She looked around the depot, which had begun to attract more people: young girls selling mangoes and papayas from enamel platters balanced on their heads, young men carrying bundles of freshly roasted brochettes, a man in his twenties wheeling a cart featuring freshly baked buns and baguettes. "Go get some meat."

"But won't I be leaving soon?" I wondered out loud.

"Not just yet, young man," she answered soothingly.

I decided it was best to relax and observe the goings on at the bus depot. Even though it was early in the morning, the heat had caused sweat to bead on my forehead. Several taxis burst through the depot's single gateway, depositing passengers and luggage near the two buses. More camionnettes chugged onto the blacktop and took up positions near the buses.

Four boys dressed only in grimy khaki shorts began to stare at me.

"Hello," I said somewhat uneasily.

The boys giggled a bit and continued their stare. My presence attracted other onlookers: a group of three teenage girls, several young men, and a tall, thin boy who maneuvered his cart in front of me. "Good morning, *Anasaara*," he said in French.

I had become accustomed to being addressed as Anasaara, or white man. "Good morning," I responded in Songhay.

The tall boy smiled. "You speak our language? For you, my friend, I have a very cold Coca." He pulled out a cold Coca-Cola from the bottom of his ice cart, opened it with his church key, and gave me the cold bottle. Already thirsty from the morning heat, I gratefully accepted the drink and paid the boy.

"Where are you going today?" he asked amiably.

"Tera," I answered, feeling refreshed by the Coke.

He nodded. "It's a beautiful town, but far away."

As the sun rose higher in the sky, the depot filled up with people: travelers and vendors, drivers and apprentices. The man who had been under the Tera bus walked toward me, carrying a greasy engine part that looked like a carburetor. I stood up and intercepted him. He was short and lean and had a small scar on his left cheek that looked like a plus sign.

"Excuse me, sir?" I said. I pointed to the Tera bus. "Is that the bus going to Tera?"

"It is," the man responded in French. "Are you going to Tera?"

"Yes."

"It's a long trip. Make sure to bring some food."

"Thank you." I said. "But can you tell me when the bus leaves?"

The man shrugged. "I don't know. Maybe we'll leave in a little while. First, I have to get this fixed. You don't want to travel into the bush with a bad engine, do you?"

By ten o'clock more taxis had discharged luggage-toting passengers near the Tera bus. A truck arrived and a group of young men unloaded from it a mattress, a bed frame, and a wardrobe. They hoisted this cargo on top of the bus and secured it to the roof. An elderly man dressed in faded blue robes led a sheep toward the bus. The young men tied a rope around it and, climbing to the roof of the bus, pulled the now noisy creature up. With difficulty they tied the struggling animal down. All this activity, I thought, meant that departure would be imminent. The aroma of grilled meat made me hungry. Thinking about the advice I'd been given, I walked over to a man grilling mutton over a fire.

"You want meat?" the man asked in Songhay.

I gave him one hundred francs.

"Where are you going?"

I told him my destination.

The man cut up the meat. He added some grilled fat. "You'll need fat for the extra energy. May God protect you on your trip, Anasaara."

I walked back to my spot on the mat, next to the old woman, and offered her some of my meat, which she politely refused. The man who had left earlier with an engine part returned to the depot.

"I'm glad to see you made it back," I said.

"This," he said, looking at the carburetor, "is all fixed. Before we can go, I need to reinstall it and then wait for more passengers."

"You mean some of them are not here?" I asked. My watch said ten thirty. "Weren't they supposed be here at eight o'clock?"

"Of course not," the man said, looking me over with a curious expression.

By eleven o'clock sweat patches stained the underarms of my new suit. My head throbbed and my back ached from having sat so long on a mat.

"You should really chew on the kola," my patient companion advised. "It will make you forget your weariness. It's true, my son."

I again refused the old woman's kind offer. In the distance, helpers secured to the bus roof cases of beer and soft drinks and several large sacks of grain. More passenger-carrying taxis arrived. By this time I was so dazed that I didn't hear the initial announcement of the bus's departure.

"That's your bus," the old woman said, tugging my sleeve. "Don't you want to go to Tera?"

"People going to Tera," someone announced through a bullhorn. "Come and get on the bus."

I thanked the woman for her kindness and stood up. As I tried to pick up my bags, four or five young boys tried to take them.

"I want to carry them," one boy said.

"No, it's me who carries them," another boy protested.

"I was here first," another screamed.

They scuffled with each other and pulled at my bags.

"Stop this, please!" I ordered, taking control of my bags. "I'll carry the bags!"

The boys didn't understand my words but comprehended my intent. They backed off and went after an old man dressed in elaborate robes.

I made my way to the bus door and stepped up into the vehicle. A man who seemed to be seating the passengers greeted me.

"Good day, Monsieur. I'm the seat arranger." He had a square face and a furrowed brow. He wore a tunic cut from a burlap sack and a pair of baggy drawstring cotton trousers. "You are the teacher?"

"Yes."

"You'll want to sit next to the driver. It's a very comfortable seat."

I looked into the man's eyes. "I prefer to sit in the back with everyone else."

The seat arranger shook his head. "Go ahead, then."

As I entered the passenger section, the heat in the bus grabbed me like an angry wrestler. There appeared to be no place to sit. A woman with a baby on her lap motioned for me to sit next to her.

As soon as I sat down, the woman's baby leaned over and vomited on my lap.

"He must like you, Anasaara," the woman said. She took out a dirty piece of cloth and clumsily tried to clean up the baby spit. Dizziness was overtaking me, but when the driver started the engine and rolled the bus out of the depot, the breeze from open windows soon revived me. After almost four hours of waiting, I muttered to myself, we are at least under way.

The paved road ended when we left Niamey, giving way to dirt roads called washboards because of their ridges. Molded in the muddy rainy season by the tread of large truck tires, the ridges then baked and hardened in the sun. The washboards, however, didn't diminish the amount of red dust that the bus kicked up. The dust streamed through the bus openings, covering everyone and everything.

Some forty kilometers north of Niamey, we heard the pop of a blowout as we drove across the top of a barren, windswept mesa that towered over the Niger River basin. The seat arranger ordered everyone out of the bus. "Find a nice tree to sit under," he suggested to me.

Fifteen minutes later we resumed our trip. Soon enough we turned off the road in the direction of the river and headed down a hill toward a cluster of dwellings at the river's edge. As we got closer, I noticed a group of women seated near some frying pans. I could smell the aroma of frying fish. A young man guzzled a soft drink.

The driver parked the bus in the shade of two tamarind trees. There was a ferry in the middle of the river, but I couldn't hear its motor. The current, in fact, appeared to be carrying the powerless craft downriver. Several men scurried to their dugout canoes and paddled after it. They soon overtook the vessel and arched lassos over each of the four poles that rose from the corners of the boat. Slowly, they hauled it to the bank of the river.

"They'll have to repair the engine, right?" I asked the seat arranger.

"Oh yes, Anasaara."

"Please, call me David!"

"Yes, David. They have to make repairs. Why don't you buy some Coca and eat some fried fish—some of the best in all of Niger."

"I think I will." As the canoe cowboys repaired the ferry's engine, I greeted one of the women selling fried fish. "Good noon," I said in Songhay. "Has your day passed well? How goes your health and the health of your family?" By then, I had learned the importance of greeting people before initiating any kind of transaction.

"All is well," the woman said amiably. Her face was smooth, round, and very black. Her eyes sparkled. An indigo homespun wraparound and tunic concealed what must have been considerable girth. "And how are your people?"

"They are well," I said. Having made my way through the Songhay greetings, I bought some fried carp and took my lunch to a bench under the tamarind trees. Several of the passengers chugged soft drinks. A short man asked in French if I wanted to buy a Coca-Cola. He was dressed in blue jeans and a blue bowling shirt that spelled out in bright yellow letters: "B'nai B'rith Lodge 497, Philadelphia, Pa."

I followed the man into a remarkably cool mud-brick structure, a rectangle about twenty by ten feet with a cement floor. The man in the bowling shirt pulled a Coca-Cola from a large clay jug full of water.

The man pointed at the jug. "That's an African refrigerator."

I laughed. Coke in hand, I returned to the bus. Shortly after lunch, the ferry had been repaired. In short order, we crossed the river. After one more blowout and a stop for an afternoon prayer, the bus finally rolled into Gotheye around four in the afternoon.

The driver parked the bus adjacent to a market plaza that bordered the Niger River. "I'm going to the market," he announced. "Come back later and we'll continue the trip."

The passengers streamed out of the bus and disappeared into the dust and smoke of the market.

"When should we come back?" I asked the seat arranger.

"In a little while," he answered.

I looked toward the market, a haze of dust and smoke infused with swirls of people, all of whom spoke languages I didn't understand. Given my weary state, the last thing I wanted to do was to plunge into that arena of tangled confusion.

"Would you like to come with me?" the seat arranger asked, no doubt noting my anxiety.

The seat arranger, whose name was Alou, led me through the market. Everyone seemed to know him. A butcher gave him meat, some of which he offered to me. "It's goat—very tender." I tried to chew on a tough chunk of meat but couldn't seem to break it down into a piece that I could swallow. When Alou became occupied in conversation, I stole a moment to spit out the indigestible meat. Relieved of the burden of meat consumption, I bought mangoes from a young girl. While Alou continued his conversation, I sat down and peeled the fruit. Scraping the pulp with my teeth caused juice to run down my chin and onto my lap. The cascade of juice added to a collage of sweat, dust, and baby spit. So much for making a good first impression, I thought.

"You bought mangoes," Alou observed. I offered him some fruit. "That's good. They give you power." He grabbed my hand. "Let's go to the bar." We left the market's open spaces and entered a maze of narrow streets bordered by high mud-brick walls. The setting reminded me of biblical scenes from films like *The Ten Commandments*. The thought of that film suddenly triggered memories of going to Saturday afternoon double features with my childhood friends. Those memories brought on thoughts of my father, who also liked to go to the movies. Sometimes he took me with him, which always made my spirits soar. My father worked too hard, but he did try to spend time with me. And then he died and left me alone in the world. "Come on, now," Alou said, freeing me from my melancholy thoughts. He led me to a small mud-brick house. Inside, a group of men sat in the cool darkness and drank large bottles of beer. A kerosene refrigerator droned in one dark corner.

"Idrissa," Alou said, addressing the proprietor. "This white man has a great thirst. Give him a large Bière Niger, and give me one, too."

The proprietor produced two very cold beers from his refrigerator and opened them. Never had beer tasted so good! We sat and drank and spoke in French with the others, who were local officials. The functionaries wanted to know about America. I wanted to know about Tera.

When we prepared to leave, the proprietor said: "This is your bar in Gotheye, David. Come back. Drink beer or soft drinks. We welcome your talk here."

At dusk we got back on the bus and finally left Gotheye. I wondered what the headmaster would think about a young teacher who had no sense of time or propriety.

Night fell, and with it the first cool breezes of the day came through the windows. The contrast with the afternoon's hot blasts made me shiver. We drove on to Dargol, a police garrison, where officers insisted on inspecting everything on the bus. They frisked the passengers and demanded that the entire cargo be unloaded and examined. The driver went into the village to drink tea with friends. Beyond exhaustion, I sat on the dirt beside the road and waited.

A policeman came over to me. "Anasaara, stand up! We are searching for guns and drugs."

"I have no guns or drugs," I said, not getting up. By this time, I was too tired to be intimidated.

"If you resist, I'll have to take you to see the commandant. You don't want him to interrogate you."

Wanting this dramatic scene to end quickly, I stood up slowly. The policeman frisked me.

"You can sit down, Anasaara."

The bus search took more than an hour. By the time we reached Tera's outskirts, it was close to ten o'clock. When the bus finally stopped at the Tera depot, a small mud-brick structure in the market, red dust covered my face and arms. Exposure to the dust had made my hair as dry as straw. The conditions of the trip had reduced my stylish starched suit to a stained, rumpled garment that hung limply from my body.

Slowly I stepped off the bus and looked into the fleshy, square face of a short, squat Frenchman. He had beady brown eyes, sported a goatee, and was dressed in a short-sleeved cotton shirt, khaki shorts, and sandals. "Monsieur Lyons," he said, laughing. "I'm Jean-Phillipe Martin, the school principal. Is this your first time on 'le car'?"

"I'm so sorry that I'm late," I said breathlessly. "I hope I haven't kept you waiting too terribly long."

"Not at all," Jean-Phillipe responded cheerfully. "I arrived five minutes ago. The bus never gets here before ten thirty."

TEN

I quickly settled into the routine at Tera's secondary school. In the mornings, I taught English as a foreign language to beginning and intermediate students. Considering the insufferable heat of the cement classrooms, most of the students were surprisingly enthusiastic. I wondered how they remained awake in the stifling atmosphere, rendered even more deadly by the repetitive drills of foreign language instruction. Despite these classroom conditions, the students were routinely polite and respectful. When I entered the classroom, they stood at attention, much to my surprise. "Good morning, Monsieur," they recited. My only problem in the classroom concerned what might be called my mildly grammatical French. Some of my more egregious errors provoked much laughter among the students. These incidents added fuel to my desire to speak French correctly.

At midday I ate a big lunch with my French colleagues. The French believed that lunch should be the major meal of the day, which translated to a three- or four-course meal. Following the usually heavy lunch, we all repaired to our bungalows for siestas. If I couldn't sleep, as was often the case, I would write in my journal or study French. In the late afternoon, I had to teach physical education, a subject about which I knew little. After a session of calisthenics, I'd let the students play soccer. Too poor to possess sneakers, the students played barefoot on a sandy field riddled with stones and thorns. How I admired their ability to run, pass, and kick the ball! By the end of a typical afternoon, the combination of heat and exertion had exhausted me.

The school campus, which was situated at the southern edge of Tera, consisted of five faculty houses, a faculty kitchen and dining area, a student dormitory and refectory, and two classroom buildings. Each faculty member had been assigned a four-room cement bungalow covered by a tin roof. The living rooms and master bedrooms featured ceiling fans that didn't work—there was not enough money in the school budget to run the expensive generator. The previous year the students had lived in the crowded dormitory. During the summer, though, the school water tower had broken down. Since it hadn't been repaired, the students had to board in town. They often complained about not getting enough to eat.

I took an immediate liking one of the other teachers, Dédé Bergerac, a burly rugby player from Toulouse. Like Stevie Hunter, Dédé was full of energy. He also drank a lot and had a hot temper. In the late afternoon after classes, Dédé and I would drive to Chez Jacob, a small mud-brick bar with a temperamental kerosene refrigerator. There we'd drink giant bottles of Kronenborg or Slavia beer. Jacob, the proprietor, was a Christian from Nigeria who had come to Muslim Niger to seek fame and fortune as a distributor of alcoholic beverages. Although he had failed in his quixotic entrepreneurial mission, his presence in Tera was a godsend for Dédé and me.

At Chez Jacob we liked to unwind by talking about French and American politics. Dédé wanted to know how Americans could elect someone as vile as Richard Nixon. I quizzed Dédé about Valery Giscard d'Estaing's noblesse oblige. We also discussed the internal politics of the secondary school. I found Jean-Phillipe Martin, the principal, a brutal, twisted man who seemed to enjoy beating the students. Dédé felt the same, suggesting that Jean-Phillipe liked animals better than people. We both agreed that our boss was a racist. We also talked about the strengths and weaknesses of our students as well as our impressions of the local culture.

"The Songhay people are proud and private," Dédé often remarked during these afternoon bull sessions. "They don't want to us to know about them. They don't trust us. And why should they? We colonized them. Many of my compatriots have abused them."

"Do you think they have hunters?" I asked, wondering if I'd ever find someone like the snake hunter among the Songhay. "I'd like to learn about local customs."

"I don't know. I've heard there are great sorcerers right here in Tera, but would you know one if you passed him on the street? Besides, why would he teach you his ways?"

"I guess I've been naive," I admitted to Dédé. "I thought that if I spoke the language, they would teach me about life here. I thought that time spent here would give my life some direction."

"But it will, my friend. It will. How many Americans have lived in Tera, Niger? How many speak the Songhay language?"

One afternoon local culture presented itself to us in dramatic form. As Dédé and I drank beer, a crowd formed in a small dusty square just across from Chez Jacob. The whine of a monochord violin counterpointed by the rhythmic thumps of gourd drums cut through the dusty air. From my perch on a bench, I could see people dancing, talking, and laughing. Then I heard a deep moan and wondered if one of the dancers had fallen or had been injured.

An old man dressed in a torn tunic and a pair of drawstring trousers came up to me. I had befriended him on previous visits to the bar, and we had enjoyed bantering in Songhay. "Monsieur David," he said in Songhay. "Come with me." He pointed toward the crowd. "You see," he said, pointing to a man dressed in a white laboratory coat. "He's interested in you. He wants to meet you."

The man, the source of the groans and grunts, twirled around in the sand and pounded his chest. His eyes blazed wildly and saliva frothed from his mouth.

"I don't want to meet him," I said nervously. The last thing I wanted to do was to interact with a psychotic Songhay.

"But Monsieur David, if you don't meet him, he'll make people sick. You must come."

The elder took my hand and led me to the white-coated man, who, upon seeing me, extended his hand. "Happy to meet you," he said loudly, in pidgin French. "I'm the Doctor."

"Pleased to meet you," I responded politely in French. I didn't know what else to say.

"Your mother has no tits," the man continued, reverting to Songhay.

The audience exploded with laughter.

Caught up in the festive moment, I decided to play the man's game. "Oh, yes, she does!"

More laughter erupted.

The man came close to me and sprayed saliva in my face. He stepped back and arched his back. "Your father," he bellowed, "has no balls!"

"Yes he does," I said resolutely, but also with a tinge of sadness. The comment painfully reminded me of my father's premature death.

The man in the laboratory coat moved away. Mesmerized, I remained rooted to my spot. The old man tapped my shoulder.

"Monsieur David. He liked you." The old man took my hand and led me back to Chez Jacob.

"You were crazy to go there," Dédé observed, when I sat down again. "I wouldn't have gone."

Feeling triumphant, I smiled and turned to the old man. "Who was that man?" I asked.

"He's not a man," the old man responded. "He's a Hauka. He's a spirit in the body of a man." The old man put his hand on my shoulder. "This may be a poor land," he said solemnly, "but it's full of miracles. You'll see."

ELEVEN

I very much agreed with part of the old man's assessment. Niger was a poor country, but I wasn't yet convinced that it was a land filled with miracles. Poor lands, after all, are plagued mostly by inconvenience. If Niger was full of miracles, I had yet to detect it. And yet, the spirit-possession ceremony I had witnessed affected me powerfully. Never had I been so mesmerized by an event. How could spirits invade a man's body? Why would the spirit bring sickness to the community? Why were the spirits both horrifying and funny? The experience made me think back to the snake hunter in Côte d'Ivoire. Did the spirit and the snake hunter share a secret about life, something not yet known to people like me? Within the ceremony's fabric of wonder, there was also a pattern of repulsion: the contorted faces, the frothing saliva, the grunts and groans. I knew right away that I didn't want to witness too many of these ceremonies.

The heat and my schedule didn't leave much time for existential rumination. After five months of "life" in Tera, I felt lonely and out of sorts. I yearned to speak English and to hang out with other Americans. I wanted companions—especially if they were female. Sensing my dejection, Dédé, who received regular visits from town prostitutes, proposed to arrange a tryst for me, but I demurred. At twenty-three I had had scant sexual experience, and much of that had been disappointing. My fears of sexual failure naturally increased my timidity.

Before coming to Africa I had naively thought that my experiences in Niger would bring me a degree of social maturity. In Côte d'Ivoire, I hadn't been able bring myself to have sex with prostitutes, and thus far my aversion to them hadn't changed.

One Sunday morning, I walked over to the faculty dining room and found Dédé, barely awake, in one of the breakfast room's canvas director's chairs. Dédé wore tight-fitting khaki short shorts and a black mesh T-shirt. With half-closed eyes, he stared at a steaming mug of coffee in front of him on a low table.

"Good morning, David," he said, yawning.

"You look tired, Dédé."

"I had too much to drink last night. Got a hangover," he said emptily. "How are you?"

"I want to know more about local women," I said rather timidly.

Dédé sat up in his chair and opened his eyes. He leaned over toward me and hit me hard in the arm. "Well, it's about time, old man. I was beginning to wonder about you." Dédé scratched his chin and sipped his coffee. "Tell you what, David. I'll make arrangements, if you like, for two girls to come tonight—one for you and one for me."

"I don't know, Dédé. You know how I feel about prostitutes."

"Yeah, but you should try it at least one time, no?"

"Yeah, I suppose," I said, unconvinced.

Time moved slowly for me that day. As each hour passed, the knots in my stomach got tighter and tighter. What would the woman be like? What would I say to her? I went into the bathroom and stared at myself in the mirror. A thick black beard gave some body to my thin, strong-featured face. My wavy black hair extended to my shoulders. The hot sun had browned my olive skin to a copper hue. Thanks to the quality of the French food I had been eating, I had put on a few needed pounds. Given the circumstances of my life, I thought I looked pretty good. Even so, I wondered what an African girl would think of me. Would she be attracted to me? I opened the medicine cabinet and grabbed a packet of condoms. I took them to the table next to my bed.

At lunch Dédé winked at me but said nothing to the others about the nocturnal liaisons scheduled for that evening. Afterward Dédé said, "Come to my house around ten o'clock."

That night I drank three glasses of wine at dinner—two more than usual. By the end of the meal, however, I didn't feel the slightest bit tipsy. I said goodnight to my colleagues and entered my house. Wanting everything to be perfect, I put clean sheets on the bed and lit kerosene lanterns in the bedroom and the living room. Quite by accident, I tuned in to a radio station in Italy that was playing Beatles songs. Everything was ready. In the darkness I sat and waited, my heart thumping against my chest.

At ten I went over to Dédé's. His dwelling was a carbon copy of my own space. Striding through the open door, I found my friend seated in his living room listening intently to Radio France International.

"Hey Dédé," I greeted him.

"Shhh," Dédé whispered emphatically. "They're playing Jacques Brel's 'Ne me quitte pas.'"

I didn't care too much for sappy French music, but this song seemed different. Jacques Brel was pleading with a woman not to leave him and break his heart. Such a sad song, I thought.

Just then we heard soft clapping at the door. In the dim lantern light, Dédé and I saw two figures, one tall and thin, one short and thin, dressed in cotton tops of print cloth and wraparound skirts. As they approached, the young women giggled. Being tall myself, I thought the tall thin woman would be best for me. I said good evening to her in Songhay, provoking more giggles.

"Please, come with me," I said.

The woman accompanied me to my house. I opened the door. We walked inside.

"What's your name?" I asked.

"I'm Fiti," she said as she chomped on chewing gum. Slouching, she looked around my surroundings. She took off her head wrap, revealing plaited hair. Dull brown eyes offset a smooth face. No facial scars cut into what seemed to me a bored, expressionless face. She plopped down on one of my director's chairs and stared at the blanket on the wall.

"It's from Tera," I said, not knowing what else to talk about. The young woman nodded and continued to chew her gum.

"Why don't we go into the bedroom?" I asked.

The young woman stood up and followed me to the large, lumpy bed. She sat on its edge and stared into my closet.

Not knowing what else to do, I tentatively touched her arm. She glanced at me and took off her top to reveal small, firm breasts. Her black skin glowed in the dim light. I put my hands on her shoulders. Acting as if I weren't in the room, she took off her skirt and her underwear, reclined on the bed, and stared up at the ceiling.

To say the least, this scene put a damper on my desire. "I'm sorry," I said to her in Songhay. "Put your clothes on."

The woman did as she was told. Her expression revealed no surprise, no amusement, and no disappointment.

"My money?" she asked. "I came all the way from town."

I gave the woman one thousand francs (about five dollars), which Dédé had said was the going rate for sexual encounters in Tera. What a meager amount, I thought to myself, for a woman to give her body to a stranger. She took the money, stuffed it into her top, and left the house. A few moments later I heard giggles in the distance as the two women left the school compound.

The experience left me feeling bewildered. Wanting to talk to Dédé, I walked over to my friend's house and knocked on the door. Dressed only in his briefs, Dédé sat in the living room and sipped on a whiskey.

"Come in, David. Do you want a whiskey?"

"I could use a drink."

"It'll help you sleep." Dédé poured me a drink. "Well, how was it?" he asked.

"Terrible," I confessed. "She seemed so bored and lifeless. I speak her language, but I didn't know what to talk about." I sipped on the whiskey and shook my head. "I couldn't do it. I couldn't do it."

Dédé laughed, but not maliciously. "What are we going to do with you, my friend?"

"I don't know."

"Things are weird in the bush."

"So I've heard."

"Did you pay her anyway?"

"I gave her one thousand francs."

"I bet she'd like clients like you more often."

"What do you mean?"

"Sex is not for pleasure around here; it's mostly for money or for procreation. Why should a woman here want to give you pleasure or even act like she's giving you pleasure? She came out here for money, pure and simple."

I shook my head and sipped the whiskey. At that moment I felt completely out of my element—so naive and inexperienced. "Are all the women like the ones tonight?"

"No. In Niamey there are sophisticated women who, like you, want companionship. I'll introduce you to some of them when we next go to Niamey."

"I'd like that."

TWELVE

Toward the end of the school year, Dédé and I drove to Niamey. Taking pity on my sorry emotional state, he was bent on introducing me to Nigerien women who wanted relationships with European men. To be quite frank, I hadn't especially cared for most of the racist French people I had met in Niger. Dédé, however, was different. This man from the south of France had exuberance for life, for experience. He embraced his life in Niger with a passion that I had not seen in other Frenchmen. Somehow we had crossed a cultural divide, enabling us to confide in each other. We often talked late into the night about our aspirations and dreams.

Once we arrived in Niamey, Dédé took me directly to Monsieur Monsard's house. Monsieur Monsard, a forty-year-old man who taught French at Niamey's lycée, had been in Niger for ten years. Among the French, Monsard had achieved legendary status for his insatiable sexual appetites. Inside his modest villa, I saw more beautiful women—all friends of Monsard, at least according to Dédé— than I'd seen all year.

Monsard had a square face and thinning hair that he slicked back with oil. He was clean-shaven, but a heavy beard beneath the surface of his skin shadowed his face.

"Welcome to my home," he said to Dédé. "And who is this young man?"

Dédé introduced me.

"Welcome to my house, David."

I thanked him and explained in some detail why I had come to Niger. Besides describing my moral opposition to the war in Vietnam, I also mentioned my newfound interest in things African—especially the history and culture of the Songhay people. "From what I've read, I can see that they're truly a great people with a glorious past."

A man with no shortage of charm, Monsard complimented my French. "The other peoples of Niger have equally fascinating pasts," he stated. "What's more, the women of Niger are among the most beautiful of the world."

Not knowing what to say, I glanced into the dining room and found ample proof of Monsard's assertion.

"Please join me for lunch, gentlemen," Monsard said to us. "I'd like you to meet some of my friends." In the dining room four young women sat at the table and talked animatedly among themselves in a mixture of French, Songhay, and Fulan.

I immediately locked eyes with one of the women. She had a beautifully delicate face framed by a head wrap: high cheekbones, a thin aquiline nose, thin lips, soft brown eyes, and copper skin offset by a subtle geometric tattoo in the center of her forehead. When Dédé and I entered the room, she stood up, revealing a tall, lean body, wrapped completely in yellow flower-print cloth. She strolled toward me and extended her hand.

"I'm Zeinabou," she said in French. Her voice was thin, childlike. "What's your name?"

In all candor, I forgot my whereabouts. Never had I encountered such a beautiful woman. She must be Monsard's woman, I thought to myself. "I'm David," I said rather timidly.

She took my hand and led me to the table. "Sit next to me."

I gladly did as I was told. Monsard and Dédé carried much of the conversational burden during a lunch of carrot salad and couscous followed by flan. The women spoke hardly at all. The presence of

Zeinabou rendered me speechless. When I sat down in Monsard's salon to have coffee, Zeinabou sat next to me and put her lips close to my ear. "Why don't you come with me?"

This statement shocked me. "But aren't you with Monsard?"

"I used to be with Monsard, but not now. We're friends. He's like an uncle."

She took my hand and looked at it. "Your hand is wet." She stood up and pulled me to a standing position. The others watched with silent comprehension as Zeinabou led me outside. We took a taxi to her house, a two-room mud-brick house in a larger compound. Striped cotton blankets covered the walls as well as Zeinabou's bed. Although a bright heat blistered everything outdoors, inside Zeinabou's dwelling dim light and thick walls kept the rooms comfortably cool.

She led me to her bed and slowly caressed my face and forearms. She kissed my forehead, eyes, and cheeks and then looked at me. She removed her top, unwrapped her skirt, and slipped off her underwear.

There are rare moments in life that are completely surreal. This moment certainly qualified. I pinched myself to make sure that I was awake. Her majestic body looked like a work of art: large, round, upright breasts, a tiny waist, slim hips, and long, thin, but shapely legs. I had read about these encounters in novels but never expected to experience one myself.

Zeinabou slowly unbuttoned my shirt and took off my belt and jeans. She stroked my chest, my stomach, and the inside of my thighs. Slowly, she took off my underwear. She hugged me and kissed my neck. Filled with desire, I wanted to kiss her lips, but she slowly turned her head to avoid that. Instead she coaxed me onto her bed and lay next to me. She stroked the entire length of my body. I ran my fingertips along her thighs. We both became aroused and entangled ourselves in a passion that I had never experienced. I climaxed quickly but remained aroused and continued to move in her. I was so excited that I moved too hard and too quickly. With a confident hand, she slowed my motion, enabling me to move more gracefully. I put my hands under her buttocks and thrust her hips against me. I geared my motions to her ever-quickening thrusts until she, too, climaxed.

"David," she said afterward. "I want to see a lot of you."

I couldn't believe my good fortune. At that moment I never imagined that a relationship with Zeinabou would complicate my life.

"Write me before you come to Niamey. I'll give you my post box number. When you come, you should stay with me."

I looked at her reclining figure on the bed and said nothing.

"Don't you want to see me?"

"Yes. Yes."

"I'll be here for you when you come to Niamey."

Rarely leaving Zeinabou's bedroom, we spent the weekend making love and talking. Zeinabou told me that she came from the tiny Fulan village of Sara some one hundred kilometers southwest of Niamey. Her family, like her people, herded cattle. For them, she said, cows were as important as people. And for them, milk was the true medicine. Of her father's three wives, her mother had been the youngest and, according to Zeinabou, the most beautiful. Zeinabou was the oldest of four siblings—two girls, two boys. When her brothers became young boys, her father taught them how to tend the family's cattle. When she and her sister became young girls, her mother taught them important domestic chores, especially how to churn butter and make sour milk. For some reason unbeknownst to her, Zeinabou's father took a special interest in her and insisted, against the wishes of his wives, that she attend primary school. And so, at the age of seven she began to learn French. Unexpectedly, she excelled at school. When she was twelve, the director of the junior high school in Say, the regional administrative center, invited her to attend classes. For the first time in her life she left Sara. In Say, which hugged the west bank of the Niger River, some fifty kilometers south of Niamey, she continued to excel at her studies, especially in French and history. She also grew into a beautiful teenage girl. Coveting her beauty, the local functionaries showered her with gifts and money, first in exchange for her company and then in exchange for sexual favors. Despite this attention, she wanted to attend the lycée in Niamey and perhaps, one day, the university. During her last year of junior high, she became pregnant at the age of fifteen and had to leave Say. Ashamed, she returned to Sara, where a local healer took her to an isolated spot in the bush and gave her abortion-inducing plants. She lost her baby but realized that she did not want to be a mother at such a young age. Having shamed her family, she had to leave. Among the Fulan, she told me, shame can never be washed away.

She arrived in Niamey quite destitute, but knew a girl from Say who worked in the OK Bar there. The OK's proprietor, a Frenchman named Duroc, hired her to wait on tables. Soon thereafter she met Monsard, who became the first of many French lovers. Her work at the OK Bar, combined with gifts from lovers, enabled her to rent rooms. She confessed to having slept around, but said she was now weary of pleasing so many different men.

"I like your face," she told me. "My people say that the face is the window to the heart. So I guess I am drawn to your heart."

I liked talking to Zeinabou. I explained to her that my family was Jewish, though not very observant, from northeast Philadelphia. I described the row house where I grew up and how I had always regretted the lack of open space in my neighborhood. I expressed to her the emptiness and fear I felt when my father died when I was only ten years old. I told her about the love-hate relationship I had with my mother. "I came to Africa," I said, "not only to avoid fighting in the Vietnam War, but also to find myself by living through a new set of experiences." Although Zeinabou listened intently as I emotionally unburdened myself, I wondered how much of it, given the cultural gulf that separated us, she could understand. How of much of her story, I mused, had I understood? Did it matter?

I hooked up with Dédé at noon on Sunday and headed back to Tera to finish out my first year of teaching in Niger.

"How does it feel," Dédé asked me, "to have spent the weekend with a beautiful woman?"

"Great," I said, beaming. "It was great. She wants to see a lot of me."

"I wish you luck, my friend."

THIRTEEN

One night a week before the end of the school year, Dédé, Jean-Phillipe, and I, the only faculty who remained in Tera, sat down to dinner. I sensed great tension at the table. The year had been a long one. There had been a serious water shortage. Even worse, several students had died of meningitis. French and Nigerien inspectors had also criticized Jean-Phillipe's administration of the school. Complaints had been filed about his disciplinary brutality. Rumor had it that he would be transferred to another secondary school or even be expelled from Niger. I silently hoped that the rumors were true. I didn't think that a man like Jean-Phillipe should be in Niger—or in any classroom.

Yacouba, the tall and dignified Songhay cook, brought a noodle dish to the table and returned to his kitchen. Jean-Phillipe, who sat at the head of the table, spooned some noodles onto his plate, speared a noodle with his fork, and tasted it.

"Yacouba!" he bellowed. "Come here!"

Yacouba strolled to the table. "Yes?"

"Will you never learn to cook noodles properly? I've explained how to do it a thousand times and still you can't get it right. In France, even a child can prepare noodles correctly."

Yacouba remained silent.

Jean-Phillipe turned to Dédé and me. "Can you believe these morons here? They're all savages, imbeciles. We should take a great bulldozer and crush their pathetic country. Then we could come here and civilize it properly."

Yacouba made a gesture toward Jean-Phillipe.

"And what does that mean, Yacouba?"

Yacouba's smile enraged Jean-Phillipe, who turned toward me. "You speak their barbaric language. Tell me what that gesture means!"

I shrugged. "I've never seen it before, Jean-Phillipe." In fact, the gesture signified "fuck you," but I refused to spoil Yacouba's fun.

"You're lying, you goddamn American."

"I'm going to tell you the truth, Jean-Phillipe," I said with calm satisfaction. "I think you're a fucking racist asshole and I'll be damned if I'll come back here to teach."

"That suits me fine."

I stood up. "Have a nice life."

Three days later I received my transfer. I was going to spend the next academic year in Tillaberi. After a year of heat, sand, and grit, I wanted a change of pace. Taking advantage of cheap airfares, I traveled to Spain and the Canary Islands, only to return penniless to Niger in mid-September, two weeks before the beginning of the 1970–71 school year. At the end of September, I got a ride to Tillaberi with my new French colleague, Bernard Montin, a small, wiry man with a long thin nose, greasy black hair, and small eyes. Montin drove a battered Citroen Deux Chevaux. It had canvas seats that looked like beach chairs, no upholstery, a weird gear lever that pulled out of the dashboard to shift, a canvas top that could be rolled back like the tin cover of a sardine can, and windows that lifted up and latched to the car's frame. As we left the paved road just outside of Niamey, I asked Montin about the absence of windshield.

"You know how it is," Montin said, smiling. "All these rocks and pebbles on the dirt road, and the big trucks. Well, my poor little Deux Chevaux can't compete. Et voilà. Breezy, no?"

During the drive Montin told me how much he liked Tillaberi. He had already been there for two years, teaching in Niger in lieu of compulsory military service. He taught history, geography, and English and was happy to have a native English speaker like me coming to teach.

"You know the last American in Tillaberi went crazy."

"What happened to him?"

"His name was Jim Bishop. One night we found him wandering around without clothes and howling at the full moon. He took some drugs, some really bad local stuff. Our drug of choice is alcohol, especially Pastis." Montin lit a Gallois as we passed the halfway marker to Tillaberi. "They came and took Jim away halfway through the school year. I had to complete his English classes." He shrugged. "It was okay." He took a deep drag on his cigarette. "Do you take drugs?"

"I like to drink and I smoke marijuana, but not much."

"Good. Maybe you'll make it through the year," he said, grinning. "We have the Giraffe Bar. We get a lot of tourists who come through Tillaberi after doing the Sahara Desert. Sometimes they're pretty interesting. And then there are the women who are eager to please us Europeans . . . and take our money. The French in Tillaberi are a good lot. We like to eat well, drink well, and have lots of parties. Some of us go fishing on the river." Montin finished his cigarette and flicked the butt out the window. "You'll have a good time."

It sounded like I'd be less isolated and oppressed in Tillaberi. I had heard that the new principal, Mamadou Amadou, was a Nigerien who liked Americans. I was most intrigued by the news about my American colleague, Darlene "Didi" Newell, a woman who, according to my Peace Corps buddies in Niamey, was tall, curvy, blond, and wild. Montin said that Didi had a rich Nigerien boyfriend who visited her on weekends. She lived in a house not far from the school. She wasn't a very good teacher, but no one in Tillaberi seemed to care. There were three other American women living in town. They weighed babies and counseled mothers on pre- and postnatal care. When I first met them during my initial year in Niger, they had seemed quite serious about their work.

"What more can you tell me about Didi Newell?" I asked Montin.

"She's very beautiful. They say she was a fashion model before coming to Niger. She knows how to use her looks to get what she wants. She smokes a lot of hashish, though. They say she's really wild. You never know what she's going to do."

"Can you tell me about the others?"

"The women are very nice, but I don't think they like French people." He smiled at me. "And then there's Bobby Claggett. He's tall and thin and crazy, from the mountains in Tennessee. He's got a camel and wanders around the bush, helping people dig wells. We like him, but his French isn't so good. He does speak good Songhay, though."

To the east lay a desiccated plain of sand and clay dotted by thorn trees and bushes. At the edge of the plain there rose a line of sandstone mountains that stretched north to south. Outcroppings of granite sparkled in the sun. To the west the Niger River carved a green swath through dune and rock as it snaked southward toward the Gulf of Benin.

"There's Tillaberi Mountain," said Montin, pointing to a peak that looked like a large black cone. "We're almost there." A dirt track meandered off toward the river. "That goes to Dai Kayna," he said. "There's a prison there. The prison in Tillaberi is for common thieves. The one in Dai Kayna is for political prisoners. They put them to work in gardens and rice paddies."

As we approached the outskirts of town, I heard the drone of a generator and the thump of machinery. Toward the Niger River, I noticed a compound of white buildings at the river's edge. "What's that?" I asked Montin.

"That, mon cher David, is the rice factory. They take unprocessed rice that is grown in this region and remove the husks. They then polish it and stuff it into sacks, which they distribute throughout the country. Tillaberi is the major rice-producing region of Niger. In years of drought, the people depend on Tillaberi's rice. The factory's manager is an old colonial called Philippe Dulay. The locals call him Monsieur Kadji."

I laughed. "They call him Mr. Scratch?"

"He's a mangy fellow, you know. His pink skin is always red and irritated from continuous scratching."

"What a crew!" I exclaimed.

"Life may be isolated in Tillaberi, but it's never boring."

The police at the checkpoint waved us on, and we entered the town of Tillaberi. We took the first right turn and headed to the secondary school, which, oddly enough, looked just like the one in Tera: barren grounds offset by a water tower, a two-story dormitory, and six one-story classrooms made of cement and covered by corrugated tin roofs. Six cement faculty villas faced the classrooms. I had been assigned the villa next to Montin's. It looked exactly like the one I had lived in the year before.

"After you get yourself settled, come for lunch. I've got a great cook."

FOURTEEN

In Tillaberi, my life took on a pleasant routine. I taught from eight till noon Monday through Friday. On Monday and Tuesday afternoons, I also taught from four o'clock to five. The school was closed on Wednesday afternoons, and I had no classes on Thursday or Friday afternoons. I breakfasted, lunched, and dined with Montin, with whom I shared food expenses and much stimulating conversation about the history of Niger.

Sometimes in the late afternoons, the most beautiful time in Niger, I'd ride a horse into the bush east of Tillaberi. I liked to take the path that led up to the rocky mesas that overlooked the Niger River valley. By six o'clock the light took on a deep golden hue and made the mesa rock glow. I loved the peaceful quiet of the bush, a silence broken only by occasional birdcalls and the clump of horse hooves on the sandy trail.

There was one destination that I returned to again and again. I'd head east across a sandy path that cut through scrub brush and occasional acacias. At a fork in the road, I'd turn north toward the mesa. As I rode upward, I could feel the late-afternoon sun caressing my already sweaty back. Underfoot here was a tawny laterite, clay as hard as rock. As I rode up the steep incline, my horse carried me through scrub, sand, and rock. Spurring the horse ever upward, I'd eventually come to a space between two sun-baked sandstone buttes. That's the spot where I'd dismount and tether my horse. Then I would sit on a boulder, letting the sun warm my face.

From this vantage, the sun would cast long shadows onto the plain that pancaked to the east. In the hazy distance I could see the fuzzy outline of a distant line of mesas. From my peaceful perch, I'd dreamily gaze at the Niger Basin that stretched before me. Fading sunlight dimmed the gleam of the Niger's waters. Cars following the line of the Niger's eastern shoreline would kick up clouds of dust. Closer to my position women, dressed in the usual coarse homespun indigo cotton wraps, would be leading donkeys burdened by goatskins filled with river water. They were en route, no doubt, to parched bush villages. Formations of ducks would fly over the buttes. When I was in college, I had never imagined myself in Africa, let alone on a windswept mesa overlooking the Niger River basin.

If I chose not to take an afternoon ride on my horse, I'd go over to Didi's house to drink beer and eat fried bean cakes. From the beginning, Didi and I clicked. Tall and blond, Didi was a striking woman with hazel eyes and a large, sensual mouth. When she taught, she dressed in a Dutch print wrap skirt and a sleeveless white or black blouse. At home she wore tank tops and cutoffs that revealed the sculpted curves of her torso. Even after a day of teaching in the wilting Nigerien heat, Didi looked fresh.

In many of our conversations, Didi said that she trusted me. At the time I foolishly thought that if I had been older and more established, she might have been sexually attracted to me. Even so, the lack of sexual chemistry between us didn't bother me too much. After all, I had a girlfriend in Niamey, which meant that "the sex thing," as a famous comedic actor would term it many years later, didn't get in the way of our mutually satisfying platonic relationship. As for her men, she liked well-to-do Europeans in their early thirties who would take her to Grand Prix races and charming country inns. She reserved most of her affections, however, for men of power. She had found two such men in Niger. One man was an air force officer who would sometimes fly a small plane to Tillaberi and whisk her away for an assignation in a place unimaginably far from civilization. The other man was the deputy minister of foreign affairs, who had arranged several times for her to travel with him to distant capitals.

As you might imagine, this behavior got her into trouble with the Peace Corps. She had already received a letter of reprimand and had been threatened with termination. One afternoon she showed me the letter.

"What are you going to do?" I asked.

"I'll do what I want," she said. "If they terminate me, so be it. I'm not going to play goody-goody." She smiled at me. "You don't have that luxury, do you David?"

"I'm afraid not." I admitted. "I need to toe the line."

"If they boot you out, chances are you'll get drafted, right?"

"That's right. They're going to have a draft lottery soon. If I get a high number, maybe I'll be able to breathe a bit easier."

Didi took my hand. "Hope you get a good number, David."

"Even if a get a bad one, I'm not going."

"That's the spirit," she said removing her hand. "You can't let anyone tell you what to do."

That was one of the last conversations we had. Two weeks later Didi simply left Tillaberi for a two-week sojourn in the Sahara, north of Gao in Mali, and never returned. After several months, I heard that she had crossed the desert and the Mediterranean and eventually ended up in Paris, where fashion shoots and rich and handsome men occupied much of her time.

FIFTEEN

Didi's unannounced departure left a social void in my life. Attempting to fill that emptiness, I became a regular at the Giraffe Bar, where I sometimes savored beer with Montin. I also started to drink beer with Bobby Claggett, the well-digger. Bobby's capacity for beer consumption was unsurpassed in Tillaberi.

Claggett was several inches taller than I was, but considerably thinner. A long thin nose sharpened his narrow face, the most prominent feature of which was a long handlebar mustache that he waxed every morning. When we had consumed our fill of beer at the Giraffe Bar and had politely said "another time" to solicitations from the barmaids, we would often go to Bobby's rustic mud-brick compound, which had a veranda overlooking the Niger River. In the golden light of late afternoon, we would look out over a mile-wide valley of verdant green that cut through towering tawny dunes. The sun would glisten on the sparkling water and the green blades of rice grasses would bend against stiff breezes. We could hear the gush of water racing over river rock as well as the sonorous call of crowned cranes flying along the river's edge. In the distance, we would see the silhouette of a man as he glided his dugout canoe downstream.

Late one afternoon, after a stint of drinking at the Giraffe, Bobby and I walked over to his riverside dwelling. We settled into two canvas director's chairs that Bobby had put on the veranda.

"It's really nice here in the late afternoon," Bobby observed in his Tennessee twang. He looked at me. "Are you thirsty?"

"I could go for another," I said.

"Well, hell," said Bobby. "I best go inside and bring out two Bière Nigers."

Bobby returned with two large three-quarter-liter bottles of Bière Niger. He opened them and gave one to me. I took a deep swig. We sat silently and observed the fading light made foggy by the rising smoke of neighborhood cooking fires. The thin nasal voice of a young girl broke the silence.

"Chenchena ney ah. Chenchena ney ah," she called, announcing that bean cakes were for sale.

As evening descended, we drank beer, ate bean cakes, and listened to the world around us: babies crying, an exchange of insults between two women, the braying of donkeys, the rhythmic thumps of pestles finding the bottoms of their mortars. In the distance, the muezzin called for the sunset prayer.

"Hey, David, I got something other than beer," Bobby announced. He went into the house and brought out a burlap sack and opened it. "Look inside," he said.

"What's in all those plastic bags?" I asked.

"That's dope, my friend. That's all dope. That's enough dope to keep us in sync for the rest of the year."

"How'd you get so much dope?"

"Didi left it for us. She didn't want to travel with it."

"That makes sense."

"Let's smoke some."

Bobby produced a corncob pipe and filled it with marijuana. "This shit is real strong, David, so watch yourself."

We puffed on the pipe for several moments. Soon enough the effects of the "little smoke" had washed away the last of an ever-decreasing repertoire of worries. I forgot about the disciplinary problem in my intermediate English class; Bobby blew off the memory of the man from Fungu village who had stolen some of his supplies.

A wisp of cool evening air swept into the compound. Struck by the munchies, we gobbled up the remaining bean cakes.

"You have any food in the house, Bobby?"

"Nope, but I got more beer. Want some?"

"Yeah, why not, but I need a big meal tonight."

"Don't fret," Bobby said. "Food's on the way."

Moments later they heard a clap at the compound entrance.

"Come in," Bobby commanded.

A little girl, perhaps six years old, strolled into the compound with two enamel pots, one atop the other, balanced on her head. "Monsieur Bobby, hawru ney ah."

"What kind of food did she bring?" I asked.

"My neighbor sends over the same meals everyday. If I'm here at noon, I get rice and sauce, usually fish sauce. Sometimes I get beef or mutton. Evenings I always get millet and peanut sauce." He waved the little girl forward. She took the pots from her head and placed them between us. "Greetings for your work, my child," Bobby said, thanking the girl in the formal Songhay way.

As the girl left the compound, I lifted off the casserole lids to reveal a large mound of millet paste in the larger vessel and a steaming portion of peanut sauce in the smaller one.

We ate with gusto, laughing here, chewing there, and frequently giggling—for no reason. Despite our considerable appetites, food remained when we were finished. In Niger, cooks always prepare more food than one could possibly eat.

"What you do with the leftovers, Bobby?"

"Don't worry about it."

"I hope you don't heat them up for breakfast."

"I might be crazy, David, but there's some things I don't do," Bobby admitted. "Nothing goes to waste here, though."

Holding an enamel bowl, a young boy dressed in green shorts stood in the open doorway. "Alsalaamey. Alsalaamey," he cried. He was a Koranic school student whose nightly meal depended upon Muslim generosity.

"Come and accept," Bobby said.

The boy approached and Bobby gave him the remains of our meal. Without comment, the boy slipped into the night.

I stared up at the stars. The effects of the marijuana had diminished but had not yet worn off. Several shooting stars streaked across the night sky.

Bobby broke my concentration. "David, there's something I've wanted to do and maybe you want to do it with me?"

"What's that?"

"You know that road that goes off just near the school?"

"You mean the road to Ouallam?"

"That's the one."

"What about it?"

"Ever wonder what it's like on that road?"

"No."

"I do all the time. You used to be able to drive a car from here to Ouallam, but you can't anymore. Bridges are out. You can't cross the wadis. They got some real isolated villages out there."

"Yeah, I guess there are some villages like that. What does that have to do with us?"

"Well," Bobby said, "I've been thinking about walking to Ouallam along that road."

"That's pretty stupid, Bobby," I said with a wide grin. "It's stupid, man."

"Maybe so," Bobby responded. "Wanna come with me?"

Although the idea was, to say the least, a strange one, it appealed to my twenty-three-year-old romantic sensibilities, which, at that moment, were intensified by a lingering high. "I'd like that a lot," I said. I extended the flat of my palm toward Bobby to receive a low five.

"Okay, then," said Bobby, slapping my hand.

"I've got a couple of days off next week. Maybe we can do it then."

"Yeah, let's do it, soon, before it gets too hot. We'll stash some of this good shit in my backpack, too."

SIXTEEN

The midmorning sun pulsed above us, but Bobby and I didn't mind so much. We had been walking in the bush for more than three hours and had yet to see another human being. This isolation made us feel free. What a sight we must have been—two blue-jeaned and T-shirted beanpoles walking on a path that led nowhere. Our broad-brimmed canvas hats protected us from the sun. Our walking sticks helped us negotiate craggy parts of the trail. Our backpacks contained provisions that would mitigate the hardships of the bush. We cut the figures of youthful albeit naive explorers. We knew our destination, Ouallam, but had we taken the right road?

The bush surrounded us. Dull brown plains dotted with thorn trees and scrub brush stretched to a horizon marked by ranges of red-rock mesas. We followed the road up and over the mesas to discover another dull brown plain dotted with more thorn trees and scrub brush. We saw no villages, no people, no camels or donkeys—only vultures.

Unafraid and unconcerned, we walked on. Why should we worry? From the outset of our journey, we had been smoking Bobby's dope.

You see, we'd finish one of the many joints that Bobby had prepared the night before, and thirty minutes later we'd smoke another. After four hours of this routine, we sat down in the shade at the base of an acacia.

"Bobby, pass me the water," I said.

"Here it is," he said, handing over a canteen.

I took a shallow swig and looked hard at him, my lip curling down. "I hope there's more. There's not much left in the canteen."

"We got some more," Bobby said. He opened his backpack and searched through the contents. He pulled out two tins of corned beef, three tins of sardines in mustard sauce, a tin of mackerel, a bag of hard candy, a box of Vache Qui Rit processed cheese, a box of sugar cubes, a large bag full of joints, a small bar of lye soap, two packets of condoms, a neatly folded mosquito net, and a compass. "Damn, I thought I packed extra water." Bobby smiled. "Guess I forgot."

"Were you smoking last night when you packed?"

"Think so."

"Were you smoking early this morning?"

"I think I was."

"What are we gonna do, Bobby?" Fear washed away the last traces of my high. "They say it'll be 115 degrees today. We've got no shelter, only a little bit of food, and no water."

"Somethin'll turn up."

"Have you seen any wells or ponds?"

"Yeah, we'll be okay," Bobby said. He lit up yet another joint. "Want some?" Bobby extended the joint to me. "You need to chill out, man."

"Not right now," I said. "We need to find a village. Let's get going."

We walked on in silence, trying to conserve as much water and energy as possible. By midafternoon the power of the sun had sapped our strength. In the distance Bobby saw a water pond shimmering in the white noon light.

"There's water, straight ahead. You see it?"

We quickened our pace through the sand, only to discover that the pond was a mirage.

One hour later the heat had completely depleted our strength. We sat down under an acacia that bordered the road and braced our backs against its thick trunk.

"This is something, ain't it David?"

"It sure is, Bobby," I said. "We'll get out of it."

"That's right." He reached into his shirt pocket and pulled out another joint. "We need to relax," he said, lighting up. "You best take a few hits, David. You're getting too serious."

I had difficulty processing his insouciance. Perhaps it was the dope. Maybe Bobby was one of those people who, no matter the danger of the circumstance, seem to emerge from it unscathed, like the soldier who fearlessly walks through a minefield knowing that he won't trip on a mine and blow himself up. Like most people, I didn't possess that kind of self-confidence. Lost in the bush, I daydreamed of Zeinabou to repress the image of my impending death. I had been grateful to be with her, and yet I knew, despite her claims to the contrary, that she shared her affections with other men. What else could explain the fact that she sometimes was too busy to see me? I tried not to think what would happen to us.

In the heat we both dozed off. I dreamed of bathing under a waterfall. I felt the cool rush of water against my skin. I opened my mouth and let the water trickle refreshingly down my throat. In the distance, I heard a voice that became louder and louder. Suddenly I opened my eyes and saw a man standing above me. He wore a filthy white turban that contrasted sharply with his square black face. A long white tunic, hanging limply over baggy white trousers, protected his torso from sun and wind.

"Wake up, mates," the man said in English.

"What?" I still thought I was dreaming. Was this truly an African using idiomatic British English on a desert road midway between Tillaberi and Ouallam? "This is a dream and you're speaking English," I said.

"No dream, mate. I talk good English. Wake up."

I spoke to him in Songhay.

"You talk my language," the man responded in English. "Very good, mates."

By now Bobby was awake and greeted the man in Songhay and English.

"You both talk my language. Praise God!"

"You want to speak English?" I asked.

"Yes. Yes. I've been for Ghana for twenty years, but Busia said he don't want people from Niger in country. So we come home. I like English."

The circumstances completely stunned me. I stared at the man, still thinking that he was part of my dream.

Bobby, who had more experience than I in the bush, seemed mildly amused. "That your camel over there?" he asked, pointing to the beast that been tethered to a tree. The camel, which carried a large load of firewood on its back, groaned.

"Yes. My camel," he said shaking his head. "You got a fag, mate?"

I turned to Bobby. "This is real, isn't it? This dude is speaking English to us on the road to Ouallam. Don't you find it strange, Bobby?"

Bobby smiled. "Not really. Strange things happen in the bush." He reached into his pocket and pulled out a joint. "Got this," he said to the man. "It's not a fag, but it's good. Want one?"

"I know this from Ghana. Let's smoke."

Using Songhay I asked the man if he had water to share.

"I have water," the man said. "You want some?"

"We're really thirsty."

Holding his joint, the man went over to the camel, untied a goatskin filled with water, and brought it over to us. "Here, fill your bottles. Take what you need," he said in Songhay. He produced a leather pouch and pulled out some *kilishi*, spicy dried beef. "Eat," he said reverting to English. "This kilishi is the best I know. Clean butchers made it."

"What's your name?" Bobby asked.

"I'm Ousmane. They call me the 'Old Zarma' because I spent so long for Ghana."

"What do you do now that you're back in Niger?" I asked.

"I get police pension from Ghana—every three months. I'm in the commerce. I want to marry Niger woman soon and have babies here."

After a moment of the comfortable silence that sometimes follows good conversation, Ousmane looked up at the sun and slowly stood up.

"Maybe I see you sometime for Tillaberi. I go there to market. Where you go?"

"Ouallam," said Bobby.

"Ouallam is far. You can't get there today. Must sleep for bush. Be careful."

"Is there a village where we can stay?" I asked.

"There is Jendi Ceri," he said. "No good place for sleep. Strangers, they don't like. Full of witches."

"Don't wanna stay there," Bobby declared.

"Go to Tondi Gusu. Maybe you stay there. Not many witches. You get to Ouallam tomorrow. At Ouallam ask for Ousmane Bari compound. You tell my people you saw me for bush. They look after you. That okay, mates?"

He strolled over to his camel, untethered it, and, as if in a dream, walked west, disappearing into the bright sunlight.

After more than two hours of walking, we realized that "not far" is a highly relative term. We saw no signs of the village.

"We're not going to find the village today," Bobby admitted. "I don't want to walk anymore." He pointed to a small cluster of acacia trees at roadside. "Let's camp there. We've got water, some food, and bed rolls."

"Okay," I said, rather dejected.

Bobby built a fire. I opened tins of corned beef and brought out two mangoes. We drank from our canteens.

"A real cordon bleu meal," Bobby remarked.

Just then we noticed a group of people coming toward us—men, women, and children. The women seemed to be carrying something on their heads.

Moments later the group came sharply into focus. "I'll be damned, David. They're bringing us food."

A thin man dressed in a beautifully embroidered boubou and a white knit skullcap stepped forward. "I'm Hassane, chief of Tondi Gusu," he said in French. "We heard that two white men were walking the road from Tillaberi to Ouallam. We have never once seen a white man walking along this road. We are honored that you have come."

"It is we who are honored by your presence, chief," Bobby said in his best Songhay. "We thank God for your kindness."

"And you speak our language! Praise God!" The chief motioned for the girls to bring forward the food. "You are tired. This food is for you. It will give you strength. We'll wait until you are finished and then bring you to the village."

"Chief, I give thanks for your graciousness. But my friend and I insist," Bobby said in a strong tone, "that you sit with us and eat. The Songhay say, 'It takes two hands to establish a friendship.'"

The chief roared with laughter. "How can I refuse someone who knows our proverbs?"

After an evening of deep sleep, we left Tondi Gusu early in the morning and walked east. Craggy red-rock mesas gave way to brown wind-sculpted dunes. We trudged through increasingly deep and soft sand, making slow progress and wondering when, if ever, we'd reach Ouallam.

Several hours into our walk that morning, I pointed to a particularly tall dune that loomed ahead of us. "That's the tallest dune I've seen."

"That's a pretty big one," Bobby said. "It won't be easy to climb."

Because the sand was so deep and soft, the ascent drained our strength. And yet, from the summit, we finally saw our destination, Ouallam, and we were energized. For the first time in my life, I felt the deep satisfaction of the explorer who, after much difficulty, finally reached his destination.

Bobby was more relieved than satisfied. "Out here," Bobby said, "people do all kinds of things they'd never do at home."

We skipped down the sandy mass. In my excitement I lost my balance and tumbled halfway down the dune.

Bobby helped me up. "You're a crazy motherfucker" he said, "and a damned fool."

SEVENTEEN

The trek from Tillaberi to Ouallam made me a more carefree person, more like Bobby Claggett. I still took my meals with Montin, who attributed my enhanced persona to increased drug use. I dutifully met my English classes but expended less and less effort in class preparation. In my spare time I drank beer at the Giraffe Bar, where my tab, which had grown by leaps and bounds, quickly surpassed my monthly stipend. After drinking at the Giraffe, I'd walk to Bobby's, where we would smoke dope, vowing to smoke our way through the considerable stash that Didi had left behind.

Every other weekend I went to Niamey to spend time with Zeinabou. When I first got involved with her, I lacked social and sexual confidence. Through Zeinabou's expert guidance, that had changed. At the beginning of my year in Tillaberi, I was love-crazed. I wanted to see Zeinabou every weekend. She, however, had other ideas. It was naive of me to think that I was the only man in her life. Although she had never mentioned other boyfriends, I knew that she saw other men, mostly French, who provided her the necessary funds to live well beyond the means of a barmaid.

One weekend after a particularly passionate episode of lovemaking, I voiced my concerns. "Do you have other men?"

"Yes," she admitted, "there are other men in my life. They are kind to me, good to me. But," she added, noticing the deep frown on my face, "I feel nothing for them. It is you I care about, David."

I had trouble completely accepting this explanation. Even so, I didn't want to end the relationship. After all, I loved being with her. By the same token, if Zeinabou could have other men, I told myself, I could have other women.

Shortly thereafter the Peace Corps transferred Bobby to Ouallam. "Can you believe it," he said to me after receiving his telegram. "I walk there for fun and now they're sending me there. They say the village people around Ouallam really need to build more wells. They're sending a Land Rover tomorrow and have already rented a house and bought me two mean camels."

"And we were having such a good time here," I complained.

"We sure were. You'll be fine, David. Besides, we can still hang out in Niamey." Bobby twisted the waxed end of his handlebar moustache. "I'm leaving the stash for you. Think you can finish it?"

"Who's going to smoke with me?"

"Maybe you'll come across some freaks crossing the desert."

"Maybe," I said, dejected.

Bobby left the next day. For the first time in my life, I realized how fragile any particular reality is, how quickly and irrevocably one's life can be changed. Faced with Niger's heat and social discomfort, I had relied increasingly upon Bobby's zaniness as a buffer from alienation. Marijuana, I realized, was but a temporary solution to cultural isolation. I refused to smoke it alone. I certainly enjoyed my repartee with Montin, but that alone did not dull the pain of loneliness. I also wondered about Zeinabou. What did it mean for someone like her to "care" for someone like me? Truthfully, I had no idea how to read her feelings—or, for that matter, my own.

One afternoon well into the spring, I noticed an old man outside his compound, which was situated on top of the dune behind the secondary school. Seated in a chair, he was beginning to weave a cotton blanket on his loom.

I greeted him.

"Good afternoon, Monsieur David."

"What are you doing?"

The thin old man waved for me to come closer. He turned toward his compound, which consisted of four grass huts. "Bring another chair," he ordered. Seconds later a small boy produced a chair. "Sit down, Monsieur David." He looked at me. "I've had my eye on you," he said. "You like blankets, do you not?"

I nodded.

"Watch how I work the loom. It's not too difficult."

"How do you get your patterns set right?" I asked.

"It's all in the mind's eye, Monsieur David," he said. He stopped his work and studied my face. "I think you have a weaver's eye."

"That's very kind of you to say, Baba," I responded, addressing the man as "father," a form of respect.

The old man, Amadu, chuckled. "Kindness has nothing to do with it. I see in you a gift for weaving. Come here tomorrow night if you want to learn."

The next night, I marched up to Amadu's compound well after sunset and clapped three times outside the compound gate to announce my arrival. Amadu's grandson accompanied me inside and pointed toward a straw hut in which I saw Amadu's form in dim lantern light. He was seated on a palm-frond mat and had placed a small dish to his side. I stooped to enter the hut and sat down opposite the old man.

"Welcome, my son. I'm glad you came. I come from a long line of weavers."

The enviable serenity of this man reminded me of the snake hunter. At last, I said to myself, I had met someone in Niger similar to Djéjé. "I'm pleased," I said, "that you invited me."

"My son, we believe that if a young man wants to weave, he must understand the responsibilities of weaving. Your gift belongs to everyone. As a gifted person, you take on great obligation. Through it all, you must try to grasp what is important."

"I'm not sure that I understand, Baba."

"You're too young yet to understand, but you will in time." He pointed to the plate, which was filled with a green paste. "That is *chakey kusu*, the magical food of the weaver. We eat this special food, which has been blessed, to guide us in our work. Without it, our work loses its force. With it, our work speaks to our great traditions." Amadu's eyes bore into me. "Are you ready to eat kusu so that you can meet your destiny?"

I didn't hesitate. "I am."

"Then eat, my son. Eat all of it." Amadu stood up and left me to eat the paste. "When you're finished, meet me outside."

It took me several minutes to eat the dense, sour-tasting paste. I tried not to think what it would do to my insides.

"Have you finished all of it?" Amadu asked me when I came out of the hut.

"I have."

"Then come tomorrow afternoon and every afternoon thereafter."

"But Baba, I'm leaving for America soon. What can I learn in so short a time?"

"You'll be back," said the old man with certainty.

NINETEEN

My sudden apprenticeship filled an existential void but failed to replace my feelings of emotional emptiness. In the afternoons I dutifully showed up for my daily weaving lessons. In the evenings I sought out local women. Montin's cook introduced me to the beautiful Fulan named Kusam, who lived near the school grounds. Hearing that I wanted local women, one of my students, ambitious for favors from the teacher, took me on nightly tours.

As the hot season unfolded, my libido seemed to increase incrementally with the temperature. Sessions with local women became more and more satisfying. I found a wide variety of consorts—a tall, copper-skinned Tuareg from the Sahara; a short, thin, blue-black Songhay from Tillakaina; a short, big-boned Hausa woman from Tessoua; a squat, energetic Bamana woman from Bamako, Mali. When I visited Niamey, I saw Zeinabou, of course.

In June, the peak of the hot season and a few weeks before my departure for America, Montin began to call me Monsieur David, parroting my many consorts. "Ah, Monsieur David," Montin would say teasingly, "would you care for more wine . . . No? Oh, then come with me to the casbah."

One afternoon, having finished a fine meal of crudités, couscous, and flan, I sat in my sweltering house. I tried to write at my desk, but the heat made it impossible. It had been three days since the school's generator had broken down. Although the principal blamed the breakdown on mechanical difficulties, I heard that we had run out of gasoline. Whatever the cause, the absence of a fan made my house an inferno. As I sat on my chair and stared at my typewriter, I heard a group of goats foraging in the garbage. They knocked over one of the garbage cans, rustled the refuse, and farted loudly. Annoyed, I opened the back door, picked up a rock, and threw it at them. They scurried away.

The heat and discomfort of that afternoon brought my sense of time to a virtual stop. Every uncomfortable minute dragged on like an eternity. My body ached and my head felt dizzy. When heat cramps gripped my gut, I doubled over in pain. As beads of sweat trickled down my back, I took off my T-shirt and aimlessly rubbed my finger across my neck. A small ball of grimy dirt formed. Like a snowball, it got bigger and denser as I methodically continued to rub. When the dirt ball was completely formed, I held it between my thumb and forefinger and examined it, wondering just how many dead skin cells the little ball contained. Then I flicked it across the room and started another rub that would no doubt produce yet another dirt ball. Such heat called for a shower, but I didn't want to wash. Why shower, only to begin sweating again as soon as I dried myself off. No, I'd wait until well after sunset, when a shower might be moderately refreshing.

A knock on the back door jolted me from thoughts about heat, showers, and dirt balls.

"Monsieur David, tu es là?" someone asked in a thin, high-pitched, adolescent voice.

"I'm here," I said in Songhay, somewhat annoyed by the interruption. I recognized Fatimata's voice. She was, indeed, an adolescent, perhaps sixteen years old. Her tall thin body and finely chiseled face reminded me of Zeinabou. I must admit to feeling rather guilty at first about having sex with such a young girl. Two years in Niger had perhaps made me a more calloused person. I'm ashamed to admit it, but I felt no sense of responsibility toward the girl, except to pay her in some fashion. "I'm here, Fatimata. Come in."

"Merci, Monsieur David." Fatimata knew only a few expressions in French, including the ever-important "Monsieur X, tu es là" and "Merci," not to forget "Donne-moi un cadeau." The desired "cadeau" usually was a gift of cloth, soap, perfume, or better yet, money. She swept gracefully into the room, wrapped only in a piece of print cloth. Fatimata, who was not a very skilled lover, was rather businesslike; she didn't want to waste time on a hot afternoon. She walked right over to my living room sofa, which was, in essence, a bed fashioned from sticks, and smiled at me. Reclining on the bed, she unfolded the cloth and waited for her patron.

"Tu es là?" she asked.

I didn't really feel like making love to her, but it would be a relatively cheap diversion on a searingly hot day. And so I took off my shorts and made love to the beautiful teenage consort. As I pumped and pumped, she remained expressionless.

"How much longer is it going take?" she asked me.

That question deflated me. "I'm finished."

"But," Fatimata protested, "you're not finished. We should try again."

"I don't think so, Fatimata." I got up, put on my underwear and shorts, and gave her one thousand francs, the equivalent of five dollars. "I'm sorry, but I'd like you to go now."

Fatimata took a quick shower, wrapped herself in the print cloth, and made her way to the back door. "When should I come back?" she asked.

"I don't know," I said in a low voice. "I just don't know right now."

"Okay," she said brightly and left.

By four in the afternoon, the hour that I taught one section of intermediate English, I felt listless. The interlude with Fatimata had drained my emotional energy. Why was I having sex with so many different women, none of whom really pleased me? Perhaps I was contributing to the local economy? That was a crock of shit. Sleeping around Tillaberi, in the end, was my lame way of compensating for the many men in Zeinabou's life. She was the only woman in Niger that I really cared about. It was hard to accept how badly she had wounded me. Why couldn't she forget about those other men? The passionless sex with Fatimata prompted me to stop seeing women in Tillaberi. During my final days in Niger, I wanted to see Zeinabou as often as possible.

Somehow I gathered myself and energetically taught my four o'-clock class. Deciding to skip my weaving lesson that afternoon, I went with Montin instead; we rode our horses east across the plains and up into the mesas. The ride exhilarated me. I returned drenched in sweat but happy about my decision to live in Tillaberi. I showered and ate a hearty meal at Montin's. After dinner we sipped some whisky.

"We've almost finished the year," Montin observed. "Are you coming back to Tillaberi? Not a bad place, you know. You could eat well with us next year."

"No," I answered. "I'm going back home. I've been accepted to graduate school. Maybe one day, inshallah, I'll come back."

"I hope you do, my friend. Even if you come back in four years, we'll probably be here. With the contracts they give us, it's pretty hard to leave."

"Yeah, I've heard about those contracts." That day, time had passed at a snail's pace. Somehow I had withstood the relentlessly searing Nigerien heat. "I'm going to bed. Hope it's not too hot to sleep tonight."

"Perhaps there will be cool breezes," Montin said.

I took off my shorts and went behind the house to find my bed.

Our cook had placed it on the upsweep of the dune behind the school. Thus positioned, I could hope to capture some cool breezes. Alas, that night was quiet and still—no cool breezes, only stagnant, humid air that made sleeping under a mosquito net unbearable. After tossing and turning for several hours, I finally slipped into a fitful sleep.

Toward dawn a tug on the mosquito net woke me. Through the gauze I saw the fuzzy form of Fatimata wrapped in print cloth.

"Monsieur David," she said, "Tu es là?"

The next afternoon I received Zeinabou's telegram, which would forever change my life.

NEW YORK 1998

Elli brought in a tooled brass platter on which she had placed five small shot glasses, a tall, thick water glass, a large cone of sugar, a tin of tea, and a small blue teapot. She put the assemblage on a low table. On special occasions, Elli and I like to drink tea—African style. In Niger, people consumed tea many times during the day, especially if they were telling or listening to a story. The Chinese green tea consumed in Niger—and in New York, occasionally—jolts the body with caffeine, transforming people into engaging raconteurs and engaged listeners. Adhering to this custom, we offered our African guests three glasses over the course of the afternoon. This batch was the first—the most bitter—and therefore required a large measure of sugar. Kneeling on the floor, I filled one of the shot glasses with tea and poured it into the pot. Using the large glass, I chipped off a chunk of sugar and also put it into the pot. From well above the table, I began to pour. Like a waterfall, the tea streamed into the large glass, creating a sugary froth on the surface. I refilled the pot and poured several more times, until the sugar was evenly mixed. Finally, I poured the tea into the shot glasses and gave them to my guests. We sipped the hot tea with great pleasure.

"Ah, David," said Mamadou, "you have truly tasted life in Africa. Who taught you how to mix tea?"

"My teacher, Amadu, taught me many things," I said. "After our weaving lessons, he'd make tea for me. We'd drink it in the late afternoon and talk well into the night."

"Is he still weaving?"

"No," Elli interjected. "He passed away almost ten years ago—from cancer."

"I still miss him," I admitted. Wasn't it amazing how good food and what could be called African fellowship prompted me to think and talk about important matters like love and death, freedom and responsibility? I didn't know Mamadou all that well, and yet here I was revealing to him many of my most strongly guarded feelings. Why did I feel such comfort among Africans?

Mamadou leaned back on his chair and finished his tea. "So tell us what happened when you went back to America?" He obviously thought it was time to resume the story. "Is that when you met Elli?"

"I met Elli much later. She wouldn't have liked me very much back then."

"And you think you're so lovable now?" Elli intoned.

We all laughed.

"I came back and immediately began my studies. Because of my experiences in Africa, my teachers thought I was a good prospect and encouraged me. I learned all about the history of Western art but not much about the art that Africans produce. I studied year after year, and liked what I was learning, but learning about art in books wasn't enough. What I wanted was to return to Niger to study weaving with Amadu. I also wanted to see my son."

"Ah," said Mamadou. "Then you concluded that Zeinabou's child was truly your son?"

"No," I countered. "I learned little about him. He might have been mine, but then again, he might not have been." I stared at the floor and spoke softly. "Zeinabou wrote about his birth and told me his name: Ibrahim. But she sent no picture and gave no other details. I didn't even know if she was going to raise him herself or pass him off to relatives."

"But you wanted to see him?" Mamadou interjected.

"Wouldn't you?"

"Of course I would want to see him."

"After I received Zeinabou's note, I wrote her many letters asking about the boy. I itched to know more about him. She wrote back, but only to tell me that she had received my money. Let me tell you, my friends, not knowing more about Ibrahim drove me crazy."

"Did you stop sending money?" Mamadou asked.

"No. I wanted the boy to have good medical care and, when the time came, good schooling."

"What made you decide to do that?" Mamadou asked. "Someone else, as you said, could have been the father."

"From the time I left Niger in 1971 I kept thinking about what Amadu taught me. He said that people should meet their obligations. He told me that I should try to understand what is important. I thought it was important to support Ibrahim. Each month I'd send a money order. One day I hoped to meet him."

Mamadou smiled and nodded. "You did the right thing."

I nodded in appreciation. "A strange thing happened, though. Zeinabou's notes stopped coming about six months before I was to return to Niger. I wrote her many letters, all of which were returned to me marked, 'No longer at this post office box.' Imagine my frustration. I would soon return to Niger, but I no longer knew where to find her—or Ibrahim."

"How did you find her?" Mamadou asked.

NIGER 1976-77

From the vantage of thirty-five thousand feet, the Sahara looked like a vast stretch of haze-enshrouded canvas. From time to time a jagged peak of granite would sweep up from the endless flows of sand, its stark gray mass contrasting sharply with the fuzzy beige of the lower surface. As we raced farther south, puffy cumulus clouds mushroomed on the horizon. The flight got bumpier. It was August, the peak of the rainy season in the Sahel, and we would soon confront the warm moist air that the summer monsoon had pushed northward. In short order, we hit a pocket of turbulence, which shook the plane and confirmed my expectation of a rocky descent into Niamey.

From all appearances my life, unlike this concluding portion of my trip, had been a pretty smooth flight. My academic credentials were impeccable. I had studied art history at Yale University, which had one of the best programs for the study of African art. At Yale, I had impressed the professors with clear writing and critical thought. My work as a graduate student, I should mention, earned me several awards, including a Fulbright-Hays research fellowship. Funds from the fellowship had paid for my plane ticket and would support one year of research in Niger.

At any moment, though, turbulence can invade smooth air. Although my professional life had been sweet at Yale, my personal life had been, to say the least, disappointing. Don't get me wrong; I had no shortage of girlfriends during my five-year sojourn at Yale. None of these attachments, however, lasted very long. As soon as a woman's behavior betrayed more than a purely sexual interest in me, I retreated, fearing that personal history would repeat itself.

Nonetheless, intense study enabled me to temporarily push aside debilitating thoughts of an abandoned wife and son. From the generous stipend that Yale gave me, I was able to regularly send money to Zeinabou's post office box. Even so, I quickly realized that money was no substitute for love. How could I have left them? Would they ever again let me into their lives? Every day I wondered what kind of life they led. Where did they live? What did they eat? What kind of clothes did they wear? What languages did they speak to one another? What did little Ibrahim look like? Was he really my son?

"Ladies and gentlemen," a voice from the cockpit announced. "We are beginning our final descent into Niamey, where the weather is clear and the temperature has risen to 103 degrees Fahrenheit. Please refrain from smoking and buckle your seatbelts. We should land in twenty minutes."

The jet's engines droned as the plane banked left and right. I saw the mighty Niger River, only a muddy stream in August, cutting its way to the south. Pinpoints of green that dotted the hazy beige landscape marked villages in the bush. Turbulence repeatedly jolted the plane. Even though fear knotted my stomach, I harbored few doubts about my ability to complete the research project. Amadu awaited me in Tillaberi, where I would live and study. In one year's time I expected to compile an enviable array of data. No matter the ultimate success of the research trip, however, the mission to Niger would be a failure if I could not resolve my inner turmoil. Would I be able to find Zeinabou? Would Ibrahim be with her or stashed away with relatives in an isolated village? If I did find Zeinabou, what would I say to her? How would I approach Ibrahim?

My command of the Songhay language enabled me to breeze through the airport formalities. I grabbed my bags and equipment, found a driver, and directed the taxi to the Social Science Research Institute, which rented rooms to visiting scholars. I said hello to the institute's officials and deposited my gear in a tiny air-conditioned room, into which was crammed a desk, a small refrigerator, a cot, a toilet, and a shower. Although I should have been tired from the long trip and the intense afternoon heat in Niamey, I felt full of restless energy. I left the room and walked a short distance to one of Niamey's major roads. Along the way I greeted a butcher roasting mutton brochettes. A young girl who deftly balanced a platter on her head offered me mangoes. A youth dressed in a filthy tunic led a tall blind woman by the hand. When the boy saw me, he and the woman sang a beautiful song and asked for alms. I gave them 250 francs.

Trucks, cars, motorbikes, camels, and donkeys clogged the roadway, which bordered the fish and vegetable market—always a beehive of activity. During the five years that I had been away, Niamey's population—of both people and vehicles—had grown exponentially. Many fully packed taxis zipped past me. After a few minutes of taking in this scene, I decided to walk toward Nouveau Marché, Zeinabou's old neighborhood. I had no idea whether she still lived in the same house, or even in the same part of town. It didn't matter. I had to start my search for her. I had to find her.

I walked by Score, a food emporium that sold luxury items. The sun relentlessly pounded my unprotected head. The dust had already begun to irritate my eyes, making them itch. My lungs burned. Near the central post office, an airy concrete structure, a taxi dropped off a passenger.

"Monsieur," the taxi man said to me. "You need a ride, no?"

I walked up to the vehicle and opened the door. "Yes," I said with relief. "Take me to Nouveau Marché."

Soon the familiar water tower came into view. I paid the driver and found the dusty, rutted side street that led to Zeinabou's house. The street cut between high mud-brick walls that separated the various compounds. At one end of the short street, a large pile of rotting garbage loomed like a mountain. Naked children played in rain puddles. At least here, I consoled myself, nothing much had changed. I finally came to Zeinabou's compound. An old woman sat on a bench under a scraggly acacia, staring listlessly at the compound wall directly in front of her. A plastic teapot rested at her feet.

"How goes your afternoon?" I asked, using the proper greeting for midafternoon.

"It goes in good health," she answered. "And yours?" She took a wad of tobacco from a pouch and put it under her lip.

I told her that five years ago I had a friend who lived in the compound. I described Zeinabou and the exact house she had lived in. "Does she live here now?" I asked.

The woman spat out some tobacco and looked up at me. "That woman doesn't live here, Anasaara," she replied. "She may have been here in the past, but I came to Niamey only last year." She moved to one end of the bench. "Abdul will be back in a little while. He can tell you more than I can." She motioned for me to sit down.

Disappointment circulated through my limbs, making them heavy, almost immobile. Sadness pressed against my head, which hung down like a wilted flower. Would I ever see Zeinabou again? What had she done with Ibrahim?

A voice woke me from my sad reveries. "Hey, Anasaara, hey."

I looked up at an old man dressed in a faded and frayed tunic. He wore an embroidered cap. "How goes the afternoon?"

After we exchanged greetings, I asked after Zeinabou.

"I remember her," he said scratching his goatee. "She moved away two, maybe three years ago. She had a little baturé child—half white, half black." He looked intently at me. "There are many baturé children. They have a tough time of it, you know."

"Why is that?"

"You know how it is. Black people don't like them because they're half-white and white people don't like them because they're half-black."

"Do you know where she went?" I asked, trying to ignore his troubling statement.

Abdul shook his head. "She didn't say. She might be in Niamey. Then again she might be somewhere else." Abdul smiled at me. "You know, she was a very beautiful woman. She had enough money to have gone anywhere—even France."

"Even France," I whispered. I stood up, thanked Abdul for his assistance, and lumbered back to the research center. Finding Zeinabou was not going to be easy.

TWENTY-TWO

The difficulty of my real task sucked the last ounce of energy from my body. Depleted, I spent several listless days in my room at the research institute. I slept, read, and listened to the radio. Refusing to leave the room to sample Niamey's restaurants, I ate food that the watchman's wife left at my door. I soon realized that in order to re-store some sense of well-being, I needed get back into the Nigerien bush. I needed to once again cross the threshold of Amadu's compound 120 kilometers to the north.

Despite this sense of necessity, malaise made me indecisive. When should I go? How would I get there? On the third evening of my stay at the institute, the watchman knocked on my door.

"Yes?" I asked with some irritation from the other side of the door.

"It's the watchman. I've brought you food and a bowl of water, Monsieur David," he said.

"Could you leave it for me?"

"Yes. But I brought two spoons. We should eat together—like men."

I opened the door. I hadn't shaved or showered in days and my face was puffy. "You're right," I admitted. "Please," I said bowing slightly, "please come in."

We sat down on the edge of the cot, a large bowl of steaming rice and sauce between us. "You must eat, Monsieur David," the watchman pleaded. He was a short, slight man with bad teeth. He wore a faded blue robe over baggy drawstring pants. We ate in silence.

"You know," the watchman said, "it's not good to eat alone."

I nodded. "Thanks for thinking about me." Caught up in my own misery, I had forgotten the extraordinary kindness of ordinary people in Niger. As the watchman would have predicted, tasty food and good company quickly invigorated me. "In Tillaberi I'll have a lot of food and much conversation. They should give me an authorization today or tomorrow. Then I can leave for the bush."

"You'll have peace in the bush," the watchman stated with certainty. "You'll breathe fresh air and walk in wide open spaces. You'll feel freer than you do here."

"I used to live in Tillaberi," I said.

"It is not far from my village," the watchman observed, "an island in the river north of there. They say that the man you will study with . . ."

"Amadu, the weaver . . ."

". . . is wise. Listen carefully to what he says," the watchman counseled. "Listen carefully."

I received my research authorization the next morning and quickly prepared to leave Niamey. Because I had no car and had not arranged a ride in a private vehicle, I would either have to hitchhike or rely on public transportation. Every year scores of overloaded and overused buses tumbled off winding dirt roads, injuring, if not killing, many passengers. As I knew from my previous experience on the road in Niger, public transport was notoriously slow. There was no set time of departure; one had to wait at the bus station until passengers occupied almost every seat. Police stopped and searched buses more frequently than private vehicles, preferring to exercise their gun-toting authority on the peasant who hadn't the means to find a ride in a private vehicle.

Deciding to avoid the bus station in central Niamey, I took a taxi to the police stop on the Tillaberi road just outside Niamey's city limits. Two policemen, tall and thin in their fatigues, stood to one side of the road barrier, a chain pulled taught across the road. A third policeman, short, squat, and older, talked to the driver of a private car. My presence soon attracted the attention of a fourth policeman. He was short and thin and carried a rifle in his hand.

"What are you doing here?" he asked sternly in French.

I greeted him effusively in Songhay.

The man stepped back. "In the name of God, here's a white man who speaks Songhay!" He turned toward his comrades. "Hey guys," he said, "this tourist here speaks Songhay."

If I could demonstrate respect for their culture, I thought, they might ask the drivers headed toward Tillaberi if they had room for a tall, Songhay-speaking white man. I greeted the other men and explained my circumstances.

"You want to learn how to weave?" the older policeman asked, a confused expression on his face. "If you can write and read, why learn to weave?"

I tried to explain how my study of weaving would bring Nigerien art to the attention of the people in America. "Many people should know about the beautiful blankets that are woven here," I told him. "They should also know more about the men who weave them. They are blessed with a gift."

The short, squat officer playfully slapped me on the shoulder. "I think you're crazy to come all the way from America to live in a weaver's compound. But it's good that you will write about us."

Several buses arrived, and the young policeman who had spoken to me strolled toward them to inspect licenses, insurance papers, and identity cards. The older policeman invited me into his office, a round mud-brick hut covered by a thatched roof. The hut's thick walls offered a cool respite from the heat. "Sit down. We'll find you a ride to Tillaberi." The policeman busied himself with paperwork. I opened my backpack, took out a note pad, and began to write.

"I hope you're not writing about me," the policeman said.

"No, Monsieur."

"How did you learn Songhay?"

"Some time ago, I spent two years here."

The policeman winked at me. "And you had a Songhay wife?"

Before I could answer, one of the younger policemen entered the hut. "There's a Land Rover going to Tillaberi, and he's got room for the white man."

"You heard the man," the older policeman said to me. "You've got a ride."

I thanked the man in charge. "I'll stop by again to pay my respects."

"You understand the ways of Africa," the older policeman observed. "May God protect you on your trip."

I put my gear into the empty Land Rover and introduced myself to the driver, a chauffeur for the Agricultural Service in Tillaberi. The man had brought the Land Rover to Niamey for servicing and was taking it back to Tillaberi. He was thin and had a noticeable facial tic. Stained teeth indicated that he chewed a great deal of kola. Leaving Niamey's outskirts, we drove past fields of millet and then entered the bush. The driver's silence suggested his lack of curiosity in me. It was just as well, for I didn't want to have yet another inane conversation about how I had become fluent in Songhay.

The Land Rover chugged up to the top of a mesa that towered over the Niger River basin. To my left I saw the Niger, a slender brown snake now, bordered by the lush green of rice fields. But the sand and rock of the encroaching desert soon replaced these sights. On the windswept mesa top, only the hardiest of scrub trees grew. To my right was the bush, a vast expanse of brown scrub plain, its monotony occasionally broken by rocky outcroppings. Small clusters of green pinpointed ponds on the plain; larger clusters marked villages. As we drove farther north, the mesas gave way to dunes.

I looked at the silent driver. What was this man's story, I wondered? Where had be been? What had he done? What would become of him? As we continued inexorably north, the landscape became even more arid, the scrub thinned out, and the dunes became more numerous. The clusters of green diminished, leaving a bare vista of sand and rock. As I traveled more deeply into the external emptiness of the bush, its bare and peaceful presence did, in fact, gradually replace the internal turmoil of my personal burdens. Thoughts of urban chaos receded. Images of Zeinabou and Ibrahim faded into the background. Focusing on the immediate future, I imagined the parched black skin of Amadu's kind face. Smiling, I took a deep breath and recognized Tillaberi Mountain in the distance.

The Land Rover rolled into the Tillaberi bus station, which hadn't changed in five years. It was still a rectangular space the size of a soccer field bordered by five-foot mud-brick walls. The dispatch office was a small mud-brick structure with two shuttered windows and a tin roof. Several boys sat on a table in front of the building. Near the table, a man slept on a bench. The midday sun bathed the empty bus station in blinding white light.

The sound of the engine roused the man sleeping on the bench. He sat up, put on thick glasses, and stared at me as I carried my gear away from the Land Rover.

"Ah, Monsieur David," he said, sounding not the least bit surprised. "Back again?"

Tillaberi's stability made me feel right at home. "Everything looks the same here," I observed.

"Nothing much changes in Tillaberi," said the dispatcher, whose name was Angu. In the noon light, his short, frail body hardly cast a shadow. "That's good and bad," he went on, rubbing his forehead. In the 1950s Angu had studied philosophy in Paris, where he had actively participated in radical politics. Upon his return to independent Niger in 1960, the authorities, fearing the power of his intellect, appointed him primary-school inspector of a district more than a thousand miles from the capital. In the absence of emotional and cultural stimulation, he routinely drank himself into a stupor. Eventually the minister of education dismissed him, and he returned home to Tillaberi, where he took the stress-free job of bus station dispatcher. He had been the dispatcher for ten years. "It's good," he continued, "because the familiar makes one feel secure; it's bad because lack of change creates lethargy." He sat down on the bench with a thud. "So, Monsieur David, how long has it been?"

"Five years."

"The French are not here until October, you know."

"I'll be staying with Amadu."

"Are you going to learn about weaving?"

"Inshallah."

Angu looked at his withered arms. "If you stay long enough, you'll learn much more." He abruptly stood up and turned toward the boys sitting on the table. "Take Monsieur David's things to Amadu's compound." To me he said, "Go now, but don't forget to come back sometime soon to talk."

TWENTY-THREE

We marched across a rock-hard plain of scrub and rock. Through an opening in the barbed wire fence, we entered the grounds of the school where I had taught five years earlier. I thought of Montin and our horseback rides to the mesas that stretched out to the east of Tillaberi. How naive I had been! The schoolyard, a rectangle of sand and stone bordered by whitewashed classrooms that looked like army barracks, was empty of students. They would return in two months, after the millet harvest. A row of cement faculty villas stood opposite the classrooms. Behind them, a dune swept up gracefully toward the north.

"We're almost there," I said. "It's hot today."

One of the boys pointed toward the top of the dune and corrected me. "He doesn't live there anymore."

Helplessly hoping for timelessness in Tillaberi, I had expected to find the old weaver where I had left him five years earlier. Some things had indeed changed here. It took another twenty minutes to walk through deep, soft sand to Amadu's new compound.

We trudged down Tillaberi's first dune and saw the fine white sands of the wadi below. Vultures flew overhead. The swollen carcass of a donkey lay on the sandy bottom of the seasonal river, and the stench of death overtook us as we entered the wadi. Not far from the donkey, children played in the sand. Just beyond the children, an old woman scooped wadi sand into buckets.

"That sand will become the floor of her hut," one of the boys carrying my bags observed.

As we labored through the thick wadi sand, we greeted the old woman.

"Ah, Monsieur David, you're back," she said nonchalantly. "Welcome."

I didn't recognize the woman but was pleased that she remembered me. "I thank you, my mother," I said respectfully.

We climbed up the second dune, slowly making our way toward Amadu's compound. The sun made my head throb. Sweat dripped into my eyes; my khaki shirt was already saturated. My moustache tasted of salt, my throat burned, and my legs felt waterlogged. But I hid my distress from the young porters. In Niger, a man is not supposed to complain of his discomfort.

Amadu's compound shimmered in the hazy midday light. It consisted of four conical grass huts. A four-foot fence fashioned from dried millet stalks provided Amadu's people a measure of privacy from the outside world. Outside the compound entrance at an opening in the straw fence, I clapped my hands three times.

We heard a scratchy voice. "Come in. Come in."

I entered. Amadu and his son sat on chairs under two tall tamarind trees, where they worked their looms.

Amadu stood up. He wore a torn black tunic over a pair of filthy drawstring trousers that at one time had been white. A black cotton cap covered his shaved head. His smile revealed only a few teeth. "David has come!" he cried. "David has come!" He clapped his hands and walked toward me.

Two women, Amadu's wives, emerged from their huts. Like their husband, they clapped their hands and ran toward me. Maymouna, Amadu's first wife, was short and round. Jitu, the second wife, was short and thin. Maymouna, who possessed a placid personality, had given Amadu a son, who lived in the Tillaberi compound. Jitu, whose personality was volatile, had given Amadu a daughter, who lived in Niamey with her husband.

"David has come," Jitu sang. "God is great. God is great."

"Take his things into my hut," Amadu told the porters. "David will stay with me."

After I paid the porters, Amadu led me to one of the chairs under the tamarind tree. Maymouna brought me a bowl of fresh milk. "Drink and refresh yourself."

In short order the compound filled with well-wishing neighbors who had heard of my arrival. Some brought me milk. Others brought bowls of rice or small sacks of millet. One neighbor gave me two chickens. Another brought me a bowl of eggs. I had forgotten the graciousness of people in the Nigerien bush. Although five years had passed, people hadn't forgotten me.

"I thank God for your safe arrival," said Amadu. "They'll bring you lunch and then you'll sleep. Later tonight, we'll begin to learn."

I looked quizzically at the old man. "But Baba," I said, calling Amadu "father" out of respect for his age, "how can I learn about weaving in the dark?"

Amadu's face crinkled. "There is much more to weaving than meets the eye, my son."

That night we sat on palm-frond mats in Amadu's hut. Flickering lantern light illuminated our faces. Being so close to him, I couldn't help but notice how time had excavated valleys in his magnificent face. From a distance, Amadu's visage was one that had been hardened by lifelong exposure to wind, heat, dust, and hardship. Closer inspection, however, brought into focus Amadu's eyes, which twinkled with such amusement that they transformed hardened features into a soft expression. By contrast, I imagined, perhaps with great illusion, that my smooth young face outwardly expressed kindness and warmth. Could such a face mask what was beneath the surface— anxiety, anger, and uncertainty?

Amadu took a small cloth pouch from the pocket of his tunic, untied it, and spilled its contents—cowrie shells—onto the fine sand.

I knew that men and women in Niger used cowrie shells to diagnose illness, uncover the past, and predict the future. I didn't know that Amadu was a master of shells.

"Take this and speak to it from your heart," Amadu said, as he gave me a small, perfectly round white stone.

I spoke to the stone and returned it to Amadu. The old man

recited an incantation the words of which I didn't understand. He looked at me. "Let me hold your hands."

I extended my hands toward the old man. Although most of Amadu's skin looked like cracked leather, his palms were soft and warm. Why did the old man want to read me?

Amadu picked out eleven cowrie shells and threw them onto the sand between the mats. He swayed back and forth and looked as if he were listening to a voice. "Yes," he said. "Is that so? Hmm." He looked at me. "It says that weaving is part of your path. You'll be good at it. It says that one day you'll like masks and statues as much as cloth." Amadu threw the shells again and frowned. "Your father . . ."

"What about him?" I interjected, feeling violated.

"He died so young. It says that you were sad. You still are, my son."

In disbelief, I stared at Amadu, for I had never discussed my father with him.

"His heart spoiled and he died."

"That's true," I said, moved by the precision of the shells.

"They say that the shells do not lie. That is the white truth." Amadu threw the shells again. "And what has become of your wife?"

"I'm not married," I insisted.

Amadu pointed to two shells one on top of the other. "That," he said pointing to the bottom shell, "is your wife. And that," he said, pointing to the upper shell, "is your son."

Five years earlier I had talked about Zeinabou to my French friends, but never to anyone else. I had told no one about Ibrahim. Faced with the truth of the shells, my first inclination was denial. "I am not married. I have no son."

Amadu began to speak. "My . . ."

"Okay. There is a woman and there is a little boy." I explained the scenario to Amadu. I talked about the telegram and my doubts about Zeinabou and the true paternity of Ibrahim. I explained how I had supported them during my five-year absence. I spoke of my desire to find them.

"You've behaved well, but your brain boils like water," Amadu said. "Lower the flame of the fire. Learn to master what is inside. Be like the weaver: focus on the thread that connects the pattern."

I didn't understand what the old man was saying, but remained silent. Weariness had suddenly made me sleepy.

Amadu threw the cowries again. "You'll learn a great deal about cloth and wood, but the search for your wife will be difficult, my son. But," he said with intensity, "you'll find her during your time in Niger."

"Will I find the little boy?"

Amadu shook his head. "The shells say nothing of him." He tossed the shells yet again, and shook his head. "You need to be strong, my son. The path to your son will be long and difficult." Amadu stood up and searched through a leather bag that hung from a rafter. He pulled out a small cloth bag and opened it and poured some green powder onto a small strip of white cloth, which he folded and tied into a bundle. "Put three measures of this powder in your morning coffee. It will give you the strength you need."

I took the bundle and once again examined the old man's kind face. Who was this weaver? How had he learned to read shells? How had he learned about plants? Amadu somehow knew about my father's demise and uncannily focused directly upon Zeinabou and Ibrahim. But the comments about the green powder seemed almost silly. How could the ingestion of green powder give me strength? My mind told me to ignore Amadu's prescriptions. My body told me to put three measures of powder into my morning coffee. Would mind conquer body yet again?

As Amadu and I ate breakfast the next morning, I put three measures of green powder into my coffee. Amadu looked at me and smiled. "Today is the market," he told me. "We have much to do."

TWENTY-FOUR

The weeks passed slowly in Amadu's compound. One morning several weeks after my arrival, Seyni and I ran errands for the family. Seyni was a fellow apprentice and Amadu's son. We walked into town and purchased supplies—yarn, kerosene, needles, and thread. Along the way, we bought ginger, dried tomato, onion, and garlic from spice merchants. We paid yet another merchant for Amadu's daily doses of kola and chewing tobacco. By noon we returned to the compound burdened with goods.

That day the afternoon heat seemed to swallow up all the surrounding sounds in and around Amadu's compound. Even the birds lapsed into silence. As people woke up from their siestas, the quiet gradually yielded to the rhythmic thump of pestles in mortars and the murmur of late-afternoon conversation. At one end of the compound, Amadu's wives prepared the evening meal. Under the tamarind tree at the compound's other end, Amadu, Seyni, and I talked as we wove blankets. I worked on a simple stripe blanket—red, black, green, and white—into which I wove geometric patterns that Amadu had drawn for me in the sand. Seyni wove a Tera-Tera Baba blanket—white stripes interlaced with intricate swirls of black yarn. A red band fashioned from points of yarn woven into the white stripe would eventually run across the blanket's center. For his part, Amadu labored on a wedding blanket, the most elaborate of a Songhay weaver's productions. It had a black background interlaced with bands of red, green, yellow, and white. On some of the white bands, Amadu had woven red triangles, squares, and even a swirling red wisdom knot, which looked like a horizontally positioned multiple-stranded figure eight. On other bands, he had sewn thick tufts of black and red yarn into the blanket.

As we worked our looms, a group of men from the neighborhood stopped by to visit. They greeted us, sat on mats under the tree, and talked about life in Tillaberi. As a respected elder, Amadu, who was an engaging storyteller, dominated the conversation. Seyni and I, inexperienced young men, sat silently at our looms and listened.

One of the men asked Amadu to tell the story of his ancestors.

"But Baba," Seyni protested. "I've heard that story so many times."

"So have I," the petitioner admitted. "But it's a good story."

Amadu stopped his weaving. "That's true. What is more, David has not yet heard it." He straightened his thin body in the chair and leaned forward.

How many times I had wished for this moment. I, too, leaned forward.

"My people have always been weavers," Amadu began, "but we have been special weavers. You see, my friends, my father's fathers came from Wanzerbé, the feared village of Songhay sorcery. There, the great sorcerers asked my ancestors to weave blankets, and so they did. Instead of payment in shells or animals, however, my father's fathers asked for magic. In this way my ancestors learned many of sorcery's secrets."

"Was it so?" one of the men called out.

"It was so," Amadu responded. "They learned to read the past, present, and future in the sand and in shells. They learned how find what had been lost. They buried magic to protect the fields. They learned how make a man love a woman and how to make a woman love a man. All of this they learned from the Wanzerbé sorcerers." Amadu paused to spit out some tobacco and clear his throat. "They wove blankets and learned magic and were happy for many generations."

"Why did they leave Wanzerbé?" one of the men asked.

"They were happy there for many years," Amadu answered. "But there came a treacherous time when the two clans of Wanzerbé sorcerers fought each other for power. Many people died, including members of my family. With great reservations, my ancestor Baru took the family east. They loaded their goods on camels and donkeys and walked for many days. They came upon the Niger River, crossed it, and continued east. When Baru saw the dunes of Ouallam, he said, 'This is where we shall stop.'"

"And so, your people settled in Ouallam."

"That is so." Amadu explained that Baru sought out the chief of Ouallam to ask his permission to settle there. "'I have heard talk of your people,' the chief said. 'You are most welcome here.' Soon thereafter the chief commissioned a wedding blanket. Observing the quality of Baru's blankets, other people sought his services. In time, people would also come to the family compound, usually late at night, in search of magic. Baru prospered. He passed his knowledge on to Mossi, who passed it on to Moussa, who passed it on Mounkaila, who passed it on to me."

"How was it," one of the men asked, "that you came to Tillaberi?"

Amadu smiled. "Ba, ba, ba, it's a long story, my friend." He shifted in his chair and put a piece of kola nut into his mouth. "The French people came to Ouallam. They liked the blankets we wove and asked us to weave for them. They gave us much money and we were happy. But the French made us miserable. They pitted neighbor against neighbor. They named a man chief who had no claim to it. Then one day, when my father was old, the French came and said I had stolen from them. They threw me into prison, first in Tillaberi and then to the east in Zinder. That was during the white people's war."

"In the name of God, Amadu, how did you get on?"

"Ba, ba, bah bap! I was lucky. God looked after me and I wove blankets for the officers. They liked the blankets and gave me a soft bed to sleep in and good food to eat. By the time I got out of prison, I was fat!"

Everyone laughed. I hadn't realized how extraordinary the life of this man had been. "So then you came back to Tillaberi?" someone asked.

After he had been away for ten years, Amadu explained, no one knew him in Tillaberi. Several years prior to his release, his younger brother, Sidi, had moved there. When Amadu stepped down from the bus at the depot in Tillaberi, he immediate recognized his brother and went up to him.

"'Sidi,' I cried," said Amadu, "'It's me, your oldest brother!' Sidi, who was about my height, grabbed my shoulders and shook me gently. 'Is it you, Amadu? You're so fat. How can one prosper in prison?'"

One of the listeners asked, "Did you then settle in Tillaberi?"

"Yes, yes. I married Maymouna, the sister of Sidi's wife, and then went back to Ouallam, where my family arranged a second marriage. I returned to Tillaberi with Jitu. We built a compound on the dune above the school. And there I wove many blankets and brought two children into the world."

"May God be praised," one of the men chanted.

"May he grant Amadu peace and health."

Having stumbled onto an extraordinary path, I listened in wonder.

That evening I sat on the mat outside of Amadu's hut and stared up at the moonless night. Several shooting stars streaked across the black sky. I had made progress on my first blanket and wondered what Amadu would teach me next. I certainly wanted to learn how to weave more complicated blankets. I also wondered about the meaning of the designs. When I asked Amadu about them, the old man laughed. "Learn how to weave first, my son. You'll know when you're ready to learn about other things." Such cryptic answers frustrated me. Two different ways of learning, I mused. As another meteor raced across the sky, a donkey brayed in the distance. I thought about Amadu's magical knowledge. Would he ask me to eat more magic cake? Would he teach me how to read shells? Pondering the full range of possibilities in the infinite vastness of the African night, my mind wandered on to more existential matters. In the emptiness of space, I saw an image of Zeinabou's heart-shaped face. I looked to her left and right, but found no traces of Ibrahim. Would I ever see her again? And if I did, what would I say to her? Would I ever know whether Ibrahim was truly my son? And if he was my son, what would I do?

"David," Amadu called from the darkness, "it is bad to sit and stare at the sky. It makes you crazy." Carrying a lantern, he walked over to me and put his hand on my shoulder. "Come into the hut."

I followed the old man inside. We sat opposite each other on straw mats, an expanse of sand between us. "Baba," I said, "you've had a life full of adventures."

Amadu spat some tobacco onto the sand. "God has blessed me with long life, but I have suffered as well. There has been sadness in my life, my son." From a pocket in his tunic, he removed the cloth pouch that contained his shells. "We must look into the future tonight."

My body stiffened. Although I had found the last session both fascinating and illuminating, the revelations had invaded my psychological privacy and made me feel vulnerable. I shifted my position and frowned.

Amadu sensed my anticipation as well as my dread. "This is a hard business," he said. "We can do it some other day."

"Let's do it now, Baba," I said softly, my stomach tightening. "I need to know what the shells say."

Amadu threw the shells and examined their configuration. He slowly lifted his head and looked at me. "The shells say that I should teach you how to read them." He shook his head. "In the name of God . . ."

"What's wrong, Baba? You look troubled."

Amadu leaned forward. His aged face glowed in the dim light. "I am, my son. You see," he began, "the shells have given you a great gift. They've already said that you will know cloth and wood. Now they say that I should teach you divination."

"I am very, very grateful, Baba."

"You should be wary, my son." He cleared his throat. "In my world gifts bring sadness as well as happiness. When the spirits give you skill or power, they take something precious from you. They gave me the gifts of weaving, divination, and magic. They took from me the smiling faces of children. In my long life, my son, all of my children, except for two, have died. My life has been full, but it also has been empty. That is the price one pays for power."

Amadu's words of caution didn't worry me very much. Clearly there had to be concrete reasons for the demise of Amadu's children. My excitement overwhelmed any doubts I might have had about following Amadu's path. Amadu had offered me an opportunity that I couldn't turn down.

Amadu broke the silence. "Do you understand what I said?"

I nodded.

"Do you understand that if you choose to learn my secrets, your life can never be completely whole?"

"Yes, I do, Baba," I answered, discounting the severity of the old man's proclamation.

"Good, then." He recited an incantation and threw the shells that would chart the course of my apprenticeship in divination and weaving.

TWENTY-FIVE

Two months later I gazed out the front-seat window of an overloaded minivan. Headed toward Niamey, the bush taxi had stopped at Sansanne-Hausa. Several passengers disembarked; others got on. We had made good progress so far. The driver had filled the gas tank (no chance of running out) and had made sure that the tires were properly inflated (less chance of a blowout). That day the police had shown no interest in checking identity papers or inspecting cargo. At Sansanne-Hausa, vendors converged on the stationary taxi. I bought some grilled mutton, took two chunks for myself, and offered the rest to the other passengers. Curious children stood near the minivan window and stared at my white face.

Lost in thought, I paid them little attention. The two months had passed quickly. I had already completed my first blanket and had started a second, more difficult work. My progress on the road of divination, though, had been slow and frustrating. After I completed the ritual of divination, which put me on the path of seers, Amadu gave me a set of cowries and taught me the incantations that empowered the voices of the shells. He said that the shell positions—male/female, client/sorcerer, birth/sickness/death—were important. "But the shells have voices," he said. "They tell you who will give birth or become sick."

Although I quickly memorized the incantations and learned to read shell positions, I heard no voices. "How can the shells speak?" I asked Amadu.

My teacher urged patience. "Your path will open," he said. "In time, you'll hear the shells." Meanwhile, Amadu invited me to sit in on divination sessions, which enabled me to learn a great deal.

During those mornings and afternoons I toiled tirelessly. I bought goods at the market. I worked on my blankets, read cowrie shells, and wrote long passages in my diary. At night, however, I had many hours—far too many—to ponder life. My thoughts invariably drifted to Zeinabou and Ibrahim. Where might they be? Would I find them? Even in sleep, Zeinabou granted me no peace, for I often dreamed of her. The dreams were always the same. I'd see myself making the fateful decision to walk out of her life. In the dream, I wanted to turn around and make things right, but a voice would say repeatedly: "Get on with your life. Get on with your life." Then I'd see Zeinabou talking to Ibrahim in a rundown mud-brick room. The boy would have hair as thick and as black as my own, a large nose (for a child), and deep olive skin. "Don't ask about your father," she'd tell him. "Don't even think about him. He left us a long time ago and he's not coming back." This speech would always jolt me awake.

When the secondary school reopened, I went to see Montin, the only one of my European friends who had remained in Niger. Despite five years of exposure to the Nigerien elements, Montin hadn't aged. The Frenchman kissed me on the cheeks and offered me a whiskey. He motioned for me to sit in the salon. We sat on canvas director's chairs that bordered a coffee table on which there was a plate of radishes and a bowl of olives. A fan whirred above us. In the background, an announcer from Radio France International read the news.

"David," he said, "you look fit, but thin. Do you get enough good food chez Amadu?" Not waiting for an answer, he continued. "Whenever you like, come for lunch or dinner." I sipped the whiskey, my first taste of alcohol in two months. "You look good as well, Montin."

Montin chomped on a radish. "Three months in the south of France is good for body and soul." He eased back in his chair. "Enough about me," he said. "You looked troubled, my friend. What's going on?"

"You remember Zeinabou," I began. "She's the one who troubles me."

"She bothers you after all these years?"

I explained the situation to Montin.

"Shit," Montin responded, sitting upright in his chair. "And you don't even know if the boy is yours?"

"That's right," I affirmed. "I have to set my mind at ease. If I see him, I'll know if he's mine." I rubbed my forehead. "I've already tried to find them—without success. You know how it is; each failure increases my despair."

Montin picked up another radish and dipped it in salt. "Go to Niamey and find them. Take my car."

"But where do I go?" I wondered, unable to think clearly. "I've already been to the old house. She left it years ago."

"Did you look anywhere else?"

I shook my head.

"Go to the OK Bar. Go to Monsard's," Montin suggested. "He's still in Niamey and is a good source of information—especially about women."

Resolved to continue my search, I left Montin's and trekked to Amadu's compound. The next day I packed a bag and carried it to the bus depot, where I bought a ticket for Niamey. We made good time—at least to Sansanne-Hausa. As I waited in the minivan, sweat beaded on my brow. The driver opened the door and started the bus. He put the vehicle into first gear and turned toward me. "We'll be in Niamey in one hour, God willing." We lurched forward and turned onto the dirt road that would perhaps lead me to my destiny.

TWENTY-SIX

As it turned out, God was not willing to let the minivan reach Niamey in one hour. After two blowouts, we rolled into Niamey's bus station in midafternoon. The midday sun had chased most people away from the bus station, which lacked its customary energy. I wove my way through the maze of empty buses, partially loaded cargo trucks, and abandoned carts to the Avenue Charles DeGaulle. The heat had given me a throbbing headache and the bus ride had stiffened my back. I waited patiently at one of Niamey's busiest intersections but saw only two taxis, and they were full. Not many people wanted to be out and about during one of Niamey's notoriously hot afternoons.

Given the absence of available taxis, I decided to walk first to Monsard's house and then on to the OK Bar. I crossed the Avenue Charles DeGaulle, a four-lane road, and walked west toward the Niger River. Here, wide swaths of sand, the site of many vending tables and kiosks, bordered a narrow strip of paved road. Tall trees lined each side of the street. I followed the putrid course of an open sewer to my left, and passed several dry goods shops in front of which someone had stacked canisters of gas. Run by Lebanese merchants, the shops offered cloth, fuel, and wide assortments of cookies, candy, and canned goods. The commercial section of the street soon became more residential. Instead of vendors' tables there were high compound walls. In short order, the sand-encrusted white classroom buildings of CEG I, Niamey's first secondary school, came into view. I reached an intersection and turned right onto a street lined with cement villas, which housed the faculty.

Monsard had spent little time tending the garden in front of his villa, which, unlike most residential dwellings in Niger, was visible from the street. Weeds had overtaken the flowerbed. Sand had smothered the grass. Flowering vines that had once snaked around the lattice at either end of the porch had died of neglect. I suppose Monsard had other matters on his mind. I clapped three times at the door.

A young woman, short, thin, and very black, came to the door wearing a swath of cotton print cloth wrapped like a towel around her body.

"Yes?" she said.

"I'm looking for Monsieur Monsard."

"He's taking his siesta," she said sternly in French.

"I'm an old friend," I countered in Songhay.

The woman smiled. "You're the one who speaks our language," she said with pleasure, but not surprise. "Monsieur Monsard has talked about you. I'll wake him." The woman let me into the villa. "Sit down in the salon."

Monsard emerged from the bedroom several minutes later. He wore a silk dressing gown. Dry and thin as straw, his hair stood up every which way. "David," he said, walking toward me with his arms extended. "Its so good to see you." He rubbed sleep from his eyes. "How long has it been?"

"Five years."

"Good God. Time flies, doesn't it?" Monsard tried to pat down his hair without success. "It gets so dry here," he said apologetically. "How long have you been in Niger?"

"About two months," I replied. "I've come to do research on weaving."

"Excellent." Monsard offered me a beer, which I accepted with gratitude.

Realizing that he would soon leave to teach his afternoon classes, I got right to the point. "You remember Zeinabou?"

"How could I forget her? She's one of the most beautiful women in Niger, my friend."

I explained what had happened five years earlier.

"I've known many men in similar circumstances," he said dispassionately. "Most of them left their women and forgot about their children. That," he said sternly, "I find disgusting." He scratched his head. "I myself have five children in Niamey." He hunched his shoulders and paused a moment. A wry smile came over his square face. "At least, I *think* I have five children. You never know around here, do you?" He took a sip of his beer. "What does it matter? I support all of my half-breed kids. They need all the help they can get around here. Know what I mean?"

I, in fact, did not know what Monsard meant. I marveled at the Frenchman's lack of sensitivity.

"Well, David, did you come to confess to me?" Monsard said, laughing.

I really didn't want to want to talk about my life with Monsard. Avoiding his question, I cut to the chase. "Have you seen Zeinabou?"

"No. You mean you haven't seen her and . . ."

"Ibrahim."

"You haven't seen them?"

"No."

"Ay yai yai." Monsard stood up. "Do you think Zeinabou is hiding from you?"

"I don't know," I said. "What have you heard?"

Monsard scratched his chin. "She's a strange one, David. She's a hot-tempered woman. She bears grudges." Monsard reflected a moment. "Did you tell her about your coming to Niger?"

"Of course," I said, finishing my beer.

"Well, who knows? She could be anywhere. She probably told her friends to say nothing to you."

"Probably," I said softly. "What news do you have of her?"

"After you left, she had her baby. She left Niamey for a year or two. I don't know where she went. Eventually, she came back and worked at the OK Bar. The last I heard she left that bar." Monsard shook his head. "I haven't seen her in a long time, my friend. You might have better luck at the OK Bar."

"Thanks, Monsard," I said, wondering if he had also been instructed to say nothing to me. "I should go." I extended my hand to him.

"Come back for lunch or dinner," he said, shaking my hand. "It will be like old times."

"I'd like that," I said as I left Monsard's villa, knowing that I'd never set foot in that house again.

I headed north toward the vegetable market, walking past a scrap metal yard on my right and the post office and National Assembly building on my left. I crossed a large traffic square modeled after La Place de la Concorde in Paris and continued north. I gave several francs to an old blind woman who sat listlessly under a tree. In front of the Rex Theatre two lepers approached, waving their deformed hands in the air. I put a few coins in their tin cup and crossed the street to the OK Bar. Outside the door, a Frenchman stood smoking. His tight-fitting beige bell-bottoms contrasted sharply with my loose-fitting khakis. We didn't greet each other.

The OK Bar hadn't changed much. The bar was right inside the door. Several barmaids sat on barstools. A bartender, also a woman, stood behind the counter. The owner, Listrac, was going over his accounts in the far corner. He was tall and fat, but well dressed in a khaki suit—trousers and a bush shirt. Two other men, probably French, drank whiskey at another table. On the jukebox James Brown sang, "I feel good . . ."

"Bonjour, love," one of the barmaids said, greeting me. She wore red satin hot pants and a black halter top. The other women wore skimpy miniskirts and skin-tight tank tops. Their black wigs featured bangs and shoulder-length hair. "What are you drinking?"

"I'm not drinking, today," I said.

The first woman put her hand on my arm. "I'm drinking beer."

I bought a round of Bière Niger for the three barmaids and the bartender.

"You look familiar," said the bartender. She was a tall, shapely woman with bright eyes. Two tribal scars that looked like plus signs made her high cheekbones even more prominent. "Do I know you?"

"Maybe," I said tentatively. "I taught school in Tillaberi five years ago," I added in Songhay.

The woman took a swig from her bottle. She nodded. "You speak Songhay," she said, switching from French to her first language.

I wanted to ask the bartender if she knew Zeinabou, but felt it imprudent to ask her straightaway. "Yes, I speak a little," I said with false modesty.

"More than a little," the bartender said. She told me how much Niger had changed. Paved roads now extended a thousand kilometers east to Zinder. Cars now outnumbered camels on Niamey's streets. A pernicious drought had killed many children. The army had overthrown the corrupt civilian government and had killed the president's beautiful Fulan wife. "That poor, proud woman," the bartender said. "She reminded me of Zeinabou, one of my friends." The woman picked up her beer bottle and winked at me. "Now I know you. You were one of Zeinabou's boyfriends."

"That's right," I said almost in a whisper.

"She had several, you know."

I said nothing.

"She's such a beautiful woman and so proud, just like the president's wife."

"Do you know what happened to her?"

"Don't you know?" she asked putting her hand on her hip. "She got pregnant and told us that the father had left Niger."

I felt my stomach tightening. I rubbed my forehead, shifted my weight on the barstool, and braced myself for a barrage of scorn.

"She wouldn't tell us the father's name, but she cared for him a great deal." She smiled demurely at me. "Even you could be the father." She described Zeinabou's difficult pregnancy and a terrible childbirth that almost took the lives of both mother and son. "My mother, who is a midwife, delivered the child. The baby came feet first. It is with God's grace that both of them are alive."

"Good God!" I gasped. "Maybe I *will* have a beer."

The bartender opened a Bière Niger and poured me a glass.

"What happened next?"

"She stayed with us for two months and then moved back to her place in Nouveau Marché. Then she came back here to work."

"And what happened to the father?" I asked coyly.

"She never spoke of him," she said resolutely. "But she did say that the father sent money to her every month." The bartender paused a moment. "Actually, she got money from several men. How about you, Monsieur, did you send money to Zeinabou?"

"Yes," I said. "I sent her money every month."

"You, then, are a good man, Monsieur . . ."

"David."

"I'm Fatima," she said, patting my hand. "And now you want to find her and see the boy. You want to see if the boy is yours."

"I need to know," I said with a tinge of despair in my voice.

"Of course you do."

"Do you know where she is?"

The bartender turned to the barmaids, who had been following the story attentively. "Do any of you know where Zeinabou might be?"

Only one of the three had known Zeinabou, and she hadn't heard anything about her whereabouts.

"I wonder if I'll ever find her," I sighed.

"In truth, I heard that she went to Côte d'Ivoire several years ago, and that's the last I heard about her," Fatima said. "She's probably in Niger, but I don't know where."

I lowered my head. "I'll keep looking for her. One day I'll find her," I said firmly.

"I wouldn't waste too much of your time, Monsieur David," Fatima suggested. "I'd tend to your work and forget about Zeinabou. The prideful ones," she advised, "are always trouble."

I gave the women tips and left the bar. How could I forget about the beautiful Zeinabou and my son? Before going to the OK Bar, I had felt that sending money to Zeinabou was the right thing to do. Fatima's frank comments had reinforced my convictions. Fatima had also said that Zeinabou had cared very much for the father of her child. That made me realize just how much pain I had inflicted on her. How could I right my wrongs? I thought about Amadu's lectures on responsibility, which settled my stomach a bit.

I walked north toward the vegetable market. When I came upon a blind man sitting under the veranda of Score, Niamey's European-style supermarket, I gave him some coins. Observing my generosity, a pack of lepers accosted me, waving their disfigured arms in my face. Children tugged at my sleeve and asked me for money. A young girl offered me bread. An elderly man wanted to sell me mangoes. Working my way through this sea of humanity, I crossed the street, made my way to a barstool at a soft drink stand, and bought a Coca-Cola. I took a deep swig. Two young men waved postcards in my face. Another man threw a pile of sheepskins at my feet. Feeling dizzy, I wanted to disappear. Just then I looked across the street toward the west and spotted Diop's African art stall, one in a line of similar establishments. I sought refuge there.

Everything about Diop was big. His head, which looked like a ripe melon, sat atop a tall body with no neck. Layers of fat gave him a smooth face. Extra-large eyes bulged in their sockets. His broad shoulders rested above the expansive plain of his chest. Even more impressive was Diop's belly. Nurtured on daily doses of rice and butter-oiled sauces, it rose from under his shirt like a round and defiant mountain. Not to be completely overshadowed, his thick thighs violently stretched the fabric of his trousers. Despite his imposing presence, Diop, who was a Wolof from Senegal, possessed a gentle soul. He smiled often, spoke softly, and treated everyone, no matter the person's station in life, with courtesy. He regularly gave money to beggars and spoiled his two wives and twenty children with a continuous stream of gifts and treats.

I had known Diop for six years. When I came to visit Zeinabou in Niamey, I would often sit and chat with Diop, who asked me endless questions about America. If it was three in the afternoon here, he would ask, what time would it be in America? Did Al Capone still rule the gangs in Chicago? How did people manage to live in tall buildings? I would ask him about the African art he sold. Diop's answers revealed his considerable knowledge of West African masks and statues. He appreciated the beauty of many of the objects and knew how the pieces were used in rituals. For Diop, though, the masks and statues were nothing more than idolatrous objects, carved by non-Muslims, which usually brought him profitable returns. "For me," Diop would say during every one of these conversations with me, "these statues and masks are wood—nothing more. I am, after all, a Muslim."

In time I bought several masks and statues from Diop, and we became friends. Diop had invited me to his Niamey compound, where his wives presented enormous portions of Senegalese fish stew, *thiebudan*, and expected me to eat every last morsel. Fear of disappointing these considerable women, whose size rivaled that of Diop, compelled me to clean my plate and ask for seconds. Toward the end of my two years in Niger, Diop wondered if I would become his agent in the United States. "You've listened to me and you have a good eye for art. You know America. We could be partners. You could sell my pieces in America."

"But . . ." I said hesitantly.

"And maybe I could visit America, too?"

"That would be wonderful, Diop, but I must return to school."

"Of course," said Diop with resignation in his voice.

"One day we may be able to do business."

"May God will it."

"And we'll write one another."

"I would prize your letters."

Seeing me after a five-year hiatus, Diop rose from the chair anchored in front of his stall and extended his arms upward.

Quickening my pace, I mimicked my Senegalese friend. We smiled and held one another's hands.

"Since when?" Diop asked.

"I've been in Niger three months."

"And it is only now that you come see me!" Diop thundered, but with mirth rather than hostility.

"I've been in Tillaberi. I'm studying weaving with Amadu."

Diop nodded. "I've heard of him, a great weaver. You have chosen a good teacher, David."

"He chose me."

"As it should be," Diop affirmed. The big man found a small chair, which he offered to me. "I read every letter you sent, David." Diop beamed. "You are a man of your word. You are a man who can be trusted."

"I appreciate what you say," I said solemnly.

Diop playfully slapped me on the shoulder. "I'm proud that you followed your path to school and that you've succeeded."

I rested my arms on my thighs and bent forward. "I did okay at school," I admitted. "But that doesn't really matter." Five years earlier, I hadn't talked to Diop very much about the intimate details of my life. Diop knew that I saw many women, but I never told him about Zeinabou. In my conversations as well as my letters I had wanted to guard my privacy. Now I was ready to reveal to him the source of my malaise.

"Good God!" Diop exclaimed. "Why didn't you tell me back then? I might have been able to do something for you."

"To be honest, Diop, I was ashamed, and I didn't want to trouble you or anyone else with my problems."

"What nonsense," Diop said. "Know who your friends are. Know who you can count on, David." Diop stood up and looked down at me. "I respect you for sending her money. That was the right thing to do."

I sat motionless, staring across the street at the blur of activity in the vegetable market. "I've been looking for her."

"Niger is a difficult place to find someone." Diop moved closer and put his massive hand on my shoulder. "Why not come and stay with me? You'll eat well. I'll teach you about masks and statues. You can work with me here at the stall. We can go on a buying trip to

Burkina Faso. Time will pass and you'll feel better. Before you know it, she'll turn up."

TWENTY-SEVEN

I went with Diop to his chaotic household, which was hidden from the street by an eight-foot cement wall. Business profits had enabled him to construct five dwellings. Each of his wives lived in a two-room rectangular mud-brick house at the north end of the compound. Diop and his two older sons lived in a four-room cement house in the center of the space. A mud-brick cooking house, small and square, was adjacent to the rectangular house that Diop used to store art. Basins and pots and pans lay here and there among soapy puddles on the ground. Children dressed only in underwear played amid the puddles. Bits and pieces of African sculpture—tall, thin, fat, and sometimes horrific—peeked out from the compound's every nook and cranny.

Diop showed me to the storage room, which doubled as a guesthouse. Although the room was dark and smelled of wood smoke, I immediately sensed the eyes of hundreds of statues and masks boring into my body. I then saw what was to be my bed, a canvas army cot on a narrow path among the objects. Ancestor figures had been stuffed under it. Above it, spirit masks hung from the wall and the ceiling. "How can I ever sleep here?" I asked my host.

Laughter rippled through Diop's fleshy body. "It's only wood, David. You'll sleep fine."

"That's easy for you to say."

"Maybe they'll drive away your bad dreams," Diop suggested. "Maybe they'll let you sleep." He put his hand on my shoulder. "You'll be fine here."

The next morning, refreshed from an unexpectedly good night's sleep, I accompanied Diop to his art stall. We walked along a dusty path that ran parallel to a busy paved road. Taxis and trucks blared as we negotiated a traffic jam. We passed the seven-story El Nasser office tower on the left and several buildings on the right that housed airline companies—Air Afrique and Sabena. At the corner of one intersection, a woman fried bean cakes. Men walked by with loads of folded print cloth balanced on their heads. A young boy carrying a gourd led a blind woman through the maze. Carrying a brass platter on her head, a thin young girl offered mangoes, bananas, and oranges. Smoke from grilling meat mixed with dust kicked up by donkeys and camels. Moving east, we finally saw the market, a knot of aggressive sellers, harried buyers, run-down carts, mature vegetables, ripe fruit, pungent spices, and smoked fish.

Diop opened his stall and found two chairs, which he placed on the ground in front of his display. "Young man," he called to a boy of perhaps nine years, dressed in a brown knit shirt and a pair of khaki trousers. "Young man, come here."

The boy walked over to them. "Yes monsieur?"

"Find us two coffees." Diop searched for some money in his pockets. "My friend wants black coffee. I'll take it with sweet milk."

"Yes, monsieur. Two coffees."

"And keep the change."

Engrossed by the unfolding activity before us, we sipped our coffee in silence. I looked at Diop and felt a great affection for him. He had opened his home to me without immediate expectation. I knew that Diop wanted to do business in America, but didn't feel that my friend's hospitality had been offered as part of an agenda to expand his operations. Diop simply liked me and did for me what he would do for any friend with a troubled heart.

A man and a woman walked by the stall. He was short and very thin with close-cropped black hair and a moustache. He wore tight-fitting dark trousers and a white dress shirt. She was also short and thin, with long blond hair and pasty skin. She wore a bright yellow sundress and a broad-brimmed straw hat. They stopped a moment to look at the objects and moved on.

Diop tugged the sleeve of my shirt. "They'll be back."

Sure enough, the couple returned a few minutes later. "Which one of you is the proprietor?" the man asked in French.

Diop stood up. "Please. Come into my shop and look around."

They looked at each other and proceeded with hesitation into Diop's stall.

"Feel free to look around. If you have any questions, please ask."

He paused and watched them as they examined the objects. "Is there something that you are looking for in particular? I've got old pieces."

"We're just looking," the woman said, a bit annoyed.

"Take your time," Diop said, returning to his seat next to me.

I spoke to Diop in Songhay. "Do you think they'll buy something?"

"Probably not," Diop said flatly. "My best business is from wholesalers. I find what they're looking for and ship it to them in France, Belgium, and America. Sometimes I sell to gallery owners. These people," he said, meaning his potential customers, "are looking for souvenirs. They're small change in my business."

A few moments later, the couple reappeared.

"You have some fine pieces, especially the Ibedjis," the woman said, referring to Nigerian twin figures carved by the Yoruba. They are small in stature and have heads shaped like chiseled cones and large, all-consuming eyes.

"Thank you, Madame," Diop said with appreciation.

"How old are the Ibedjis?" the man asked.

"I can't say, exactly." Diop got up, went to his stall, and brought back one of the figurines in question. He caressed the piece. "You can see," he said, "that the pieces are old and well-carved." He remained standing.

"But you don't know how old?" the woman asked.

"Do you have papers for your pieces?" the man asked, before Diop had a chance to answer the woman.

"I buy the pieces from the people who carve them," Diop said authoritatively. "They don't read or write." He handed the figurine to the woman. "Look at the piece, Madame. It's beautifully carved." He sat down next to me.

The woman caressed the figurine and turned to the man. "I've been looking for an Ibedji."

The man looked at the figurine that rested comfortably in the woman's bony hands. "Is the piece real or fake?" he asked.

Diop cleared his throat and shifted his weight. "Monsieur," he said calmly. "I collect and sell only authentic pieces."

The man put his hands in his pockets and shrugged his shoulders. "Well, yes. But has the piece been used?"

"What do you mean?" Diop asked.

"Has it been used in ritual? Has it received sacrificial blood?"

Diop stood up and towered over the short, frail man. "These are well-carved authentic pieces, Monsieur."

"How much?" he asked.

Diop scratched his chin. "You know, you are both very knowledgeable. Do you own a gallery?" he asked, to disingenuously flatter people whom he considered ignorant and insulting.

"No," the woman said stiffly. "We're collectors."

"We've been collecting African art for years," the man added in a pompous tone.

"Considering your expertise," he said, "I'll offer you a good price." He watched the woman caress the piece. "That piece is one of my best. I'd normally sell it for twenty thousand francs, but I'll give it to you for fifteen thousand."

"Without papers," the woman said, "that's far too much."

Diop shrugged and laughed. "Forgive me, Madame. But if I sold it for less I'd have to give it to you at cost. That, my friends, is not good business."

"Since the piece doesn't have papers, we'll offer ten thousand francs."

Diop shook the man's hand. "The Ibedji is yours," he said, smiling. "I hope you enjoy it."

The woman continued to fondle the figure.

After paying Diop, the man kissed the woman on the cheek. "This is just what we were looking for."

Diop went into his stall, retrieved a plastic bag, and gave it to them.

"That's okay," the woman said. "I'll put it in my purse."

"As you wish, Madame."

They bade Diop a self-satisfied goodbye and walked away.

"How can you tolerate people like that?" I asked, once the couple was out of earshot.

"When people treat you like a fool," Diop said, "they make fools of themselves. I played their game and made a good sale. In life—and business—you sometimes need to bury your pride. Otherwise, things can get out of hand."

Diop's comment made me think of how Zeinabou's stubborn pride had created a seemingly impenetrable barrier between us. I knew my precipitous departure was a serious mistake. But hadn't I sent her money every month for five years? Didn't that count for something? And now I'd come back to Niger to make amends, to set things straight. Would she ever forgive me? Would she ever allow me to meet Ibrahim? For me things had certainly gotten out of hand. Pride and, yes, arrogance had changed the substance of my life. "How do you bury your pride?" I asked Diop.

Diop shook his head. "Nothing can be more difficult. You must be on guard all the time. You must try to be humble. You must realize that your life is fleeting. Everyone, tall and short, rich and poor, suffers the same fate. The poorest of beggars can lead a life sweeter than that of the richest of merchants. God gave me a head for business. I'm honest and I have two good women as wives. I've got a compound full of children who eat well every day. I'm thankful for what I've got. But," he said looking skyward, "it can all change in an instant, can it not?"

TWENTY-EIGHT

One week later, Diop woke me before dawn to announce our imminent departure for Burkina Faso.

"We're going to buy Lobi, Gurunsi, and Senufo pieces," Diop said, referring to art carved by peoples along the southern border of Burkina Faso. "I have a contact in Kanchari, just over the Niger-Burkina border." He shook me hard, for I had become blissfully accustomed to sleeping soundly in Diop's storage room. "Wake up. We have to get an early start and head west."

Diop had risen well before sunrise and brought back to his compound a small Peugeot truck he had borrowed from one of his Senegalese compatriots. The truck, which he had used many times before, had the heavy-duty struts needed to negotiate the nearly impassable dirt road that connected Niamey to Kanchari.

After I quickly put on a pair of loose-fitting khaki trousers and a T-shirt, we slipped out of the compound. On the street, we ordered some coffee, Nescafé mixed with sweetened evaporated milk, which I put into a thermos. As sharp blades of sunlight cut through the morning dust, Diop started the truck. We drove through the sleepy city. Beggars slept on flattened cardboard boxes they had placed along the roadway. A merchant opened the tin door of his dry goods shop. An old woman, as spare and dry as a dying plant, stared blankly at the sky as she defecated into an open sewer. Donkeys brayed, infants cried, truck engines droned, and car horns honked. Diop skillfully negotiated a morning traffic pattern complicated by dazed pedestrians, belligerent camels, and reckless drivers.

"Driving here is crazy," Diop complained. "Once we get over the bridge," he said, referring to the John F. Kennedy Bridge, which spanned the Niger River, "traffic will thin out." We rounded a curve in the road and headed for the bridge—two lanes clogged with cars, trucks, camels, and donkeys. Beyond the bridge, three majestic mesas rose like pyramids from the parched plain. Seeing them reminded me of my crazy friend Bobby Claggett. As paved road gave way to rutted washboards, I remembered careening down the same road with Bobby in 1970. Bobby had "borrowed" the battered Peace Corps jeep and had invited me on a journey of discovery. "Let's see if this old Jeep can make it up to the top of the three mesas," Bobby had said. The reefer we had smoked made us daring and reckless. We almost made it to the top, but because we nearly turned over three times, we gave up. On the way back, we suffered two flat tires and an overheated radiator. While hanging out with African mechanics, who slowly put the jeep back together, we learned the lesson of patience.

The memories made me smile with pleasure as I looked back toward Niamey. A cloud of dust kicked up by Diop's truck obscured the city skyline. To our left and right, small villages had been constructed. A large encampment of Tuareg nomads, the famous blue men of the Sahara, came into view on the left. A knot of tethered camels stood in the center of a swirl of tents and shanties crafted from scraps of discarded metal. A woman clothed in homespun cloth dyed indigo blue stood at the edge of the road, holding the hand of a child who wore only a string of beads around her waist. An old withered man, dressed in a dirty white tunic, sat behind a pile of firewood he had collected. Would he sell enough of it to feed his family that night? The road turned north for several kilometers, winding its way among dune palms and acacias. The stumps of recently harvested millet plants marked fields that hugged both sides of the road. By the time the road turned back toward the west, the three mesas loomed behind us. We climbed up a hill and drove along a high, barren plateau, whose unremitting bleakness was broken here and there by sandstone buttes. A network of gullies, lined with spotty scrub and scraggly acacias, cut through the rock-hard clay. This land supported no crops, no livestock, and no villages.

The sun pulsed hot in a cloudless, blanched sky. Eventually, the scenery changed from plateau to rolling dunes. Here water rushed down gullies and pooled in water holes. Millet grew in the sandy soil, and we saw several straw field huts perched like sugar cones along the road. As we proceeded west, we noticed several clusters of huts—the villages of millet farmers. A herd of cattle crossed the road in front of us. A young boy, tall and thin as a millet stalk, walked behind the herd. He waved a hardwood baton to direct the cattle safely across the roadway.

"We must be getting close to Torodi. There are a lot of Fulan herders around here," Diop said.

Mention of Fulan herders reminded me once again of Zeinabou, herself the daughter of Fulan herders. Her village was close to Torodi, and she probably had relatives who lived there. The Fulan were a proud people. They liked herding and the freedom of the deep bush. For them milk was the remedy for all of life's ills. What's more, they considered themselves superior to the lowly farming peoples who tilled the soils of sedentary villages. Neither reason nor force had diminished their pride. "Yeah, this is Fulan country," I said. "Zeinabou's people are from a village near here."

Sunlight mixed with dust to create a midmorning haze. In the distance we saw Torodi, a shimmering village of mud-brick houses and straw huts that bordered the road. A young boy led a donkey laden with bundled firewood. A clay jug balanced on her head, a tall, thin, copper-skinned Fulan girl strolled gracefully toward the town. Seated on a crude wooden cart, a man smacked a donkey with a hardwood cane. "It must be market day," Diop observed. "Here you get the best Fulan butter in all of Niger."

Amid smoke and dust, the market, a colorful tangle of people, livestock, vegetables, and spices, appeared to our left. "Stop here," I said as we came upon a man cooking kabobs on a grill. He had sprinkled peanut flour on the meat and was basting the skewers with peanut oil. I paid for two kabobs and we were on our way. Ahead of us a stiff breeze whipped a Nigerien flag that hung from a pole in front of a whitewashed concrete building. Several meters farther along loomed the customs office, a square one-room mud-brick structure. A flimsy wood barrier blocked the road—the last Nigerien outpost until the border. Diop drove up to the barrier, retrieved his papers from the glove compartment, and got out of the car. The customs officer, a large doughy-looking man somewhere in his thirties, sat passively on a battered metal chair under one of two trees that shaded his office. He wore green army fatigues, shiny black boots, and a red beret. After they exchanged pleasantries, Diop handed the man an envelope. The officer got up and invited Diop into his office. Moments later they emerged, smiling, and strolled toward the truck. The man raised the barrier, and we drove west toward Burkina Faso.

Diop winked at me. "I've been doing business with Idrissa for more than five years now. He is one of the hidden costs," he explained, referring to the envelope he had given to the customs officer, "of transporting art across the border."

"Dash," I replied, using the pidgin English term for bribe, "is just part of life."

Diop smiled and looked at me. "Yes, it is. You've got it in America, don't you?"

"Oh yes."

"Here, it makes things easier. Men like Idrissa depend on the extra income." Diop pointed ahead toward the edge of the escarpment. "We'll soon be leaving Fulan country."

At the escarpment's precipice, we looked out over the vast country below. There was no dust haze here, only clear bright light. The green leaves of cottonwoods dappled a vast brown plain of elephant grass. In the distance, clouds of smoke formed above brush fires. The country reminded me of Bouaké in Côte d'Ivoire. The image of Djéjé, the snake hunter who had so impressed me many years earlier, came to my mind.

Diop put the truck into low gear for the treacherous descent to the grasslands. Hairpin curves and ruts in the road slowed our progress. Five kilometers beyond the escarpment, we came upon Dolo, a small village. People there lived in complexes of thatched-roofed mud-brick huts that extended from the village center like the numbers on a clock. A cement church stood at the very center of Dolo. A market area, now empty, faced the church. "Tomorrow is market day," Diop observed. "The millet beer here is good."

I studied the people milling about town. They were uniformly short and chunky and had broad, almost square faces. Three tribal scars lined the cheeks of several men. The smiles of women revealed teeth that had been filed into sharp points. In ten kilometers the world had drastically changed: from Muslim to Catholic; from tall, thin Fulan to short, square Gurmantché; from dusty steppe to clear grassland. Africa, I thought in wonder, is truly defined by its diversity.

Diop stopped the car in front of a short, round-faced woman who stood behind two large cast-iron pots. Long ladle in hand, she stirred one of the pots. Two men sat on a bench and ate rice and sauce from plastic bowls. "Let's sample the local cuisine, David," Diop suggested. "I'm hungry."

"Good idea."

"Hello, Madame Kapale," Diop said, greeting the woman. "How is the sauce today?"

"The meat is very tender today, Monsieur Diop."

"Two bowls, then, for me and my friend."

Madame Kapale spooned heaping mounds of rice into the two bowls and then covered them with steaming sauce. She made sure we both received several chunks of meat.

Like the other men, we sat on the bench and ate from our bowls.

"Diop," I said, "this is one of best sauces I have ever tasted in Africa."

Diop smiled. "The Gurmantché know their sauces."

When I complimented her on a fine sauce, Madame Kapale beamed. "Come again, my friends," she said in French.

We drove on toward the border, the road a narrow path that cut through a forest of elephant grass. I turned toward Diop. "By the way, what kind of meat did we just eat?"

Diop smiled broadly. "Bush rat. Much better than city rat, don't you think?"

"Yes, of course," I said, trying to keep the meal in my stomach.

In the distance a large clearing in the grassland marked Kanchari, the border town where Diop intended to do business. Crude tables loaded with offerings of fruit, vegetables, and grilled meat lined the wide dirt road that led into town. A pair of large whitewashed cement buildings stood out among the surrounding mud-brick bungalows and huts. The Burkinabe flag identified one of them as the customs building. Next to it, a Stella Artois Beer sign distinguished the Bar Bon Temps, a considerably larger structure than the customs office.

Diop headed for the bar. Following my mentor, I wondered why Diop hadn't first checked in with the customs people. I had my answer moments later when Diop introduced me to Gregoire Kankare, the chief customs officer, who was seated at a table in the bar. Gregoire was similar to Diop in size: large head, bulging eyes, full cheeks, bull neck, wide chest, expansive belly, thick legs. His uniform, a size too small, made him seem even bigger. Diop gave Gregoire an envelope.

"Good to see you, Diop," he said. He looked at me and extended his hand. "Let me buy you and your friend a beer." Gregoire slapped his leg. "I forgot about you, Diop. You don't drink. Let me buy you a Coca."

"I'll have a beer," I chimed in.

"Ah," said the massive Gregoire, "a man like me."

We sipped our drinks. Gregoire made quick work of his liter bottle and ordered another.

"Gregoire," Diop said, "we're going to be doing business at Talou Fall's. We'll be back in maybe one or two hours."

Gregoire smiled at us. "I'm not going anywhere. Stop by when you get ready to leave."

I followed Diop through a series of garbage-strewn streets that wove through Kanchari's neighborhoods. Low walls revealed large compounds of mud-brick huts with grass roofs. On the dirt streets, several naked children chased after one another, and a group of barefoot young boys played soccer. A bone-thin girl asked me for money. "Please, Monsieur," she said in puerile French, "I haven't eaten in two days."

I gave her lunch money. "People are horribly poor here," I observed.

"It's bad," Diop agreed. "They lack Muslim industry and generosity." Diop led me to a square mud-brick structure featuring a bright red "Buvez Coca Cola" sign above the doorway. It was Talou Fall's dry goods shop, which seemed empty.

"Hey Talou, hey," Diop called out to his compatriot in Wolof, the language they shared. The shop was dark, dank, and crammed with boxes of sugar, soap, hard candy, and batteries. A red cooler stood in one corner.

A moment later Talou ducked through the doorway cut into the back wall and came into the shop. He was exceedingly tall and thin and very black. He greeted Diop, who immediately introduced me.

"The wood is in the compound," he announced. "Follow me." Talou spent much of his time in the bush in search of African art, traveling to small villages in Côte d'Ivoire to buy statues and masks from Senufo and Baulé carvers. In Burkina Faso, he found art in Lobi and Gurunsi country—hundreds of kilometers southwest of Kanchari along the borders of Togo and Ghana. His wife, a local woman, ran the dry goods shop.

"And how is your wife?" Diop asked his friend.

"In God's name, she is in good health," Talou responded in French so that I, too, could follow the conversation. "Because the children are in school today, she's visiting her sister's village."

We entered a courtyard with three rectangular mud-brick houses connected to the compound's back wall. Two tall mud-brick granaries rose like large beehives in one corner. In the compound's center, pegs had been hammered into the ground to tether livestock. "We have two cows, four sheep, and five goats," he said proudly.

Talou took us to the smallest of the houses. It smelled of smoke and insecticide. In the darkness I noticed shelves stuffed with boxes and bags. A four-foot Senufo hornbill statue stood in the corner; it was a mythic bird with clipped wings, thick legs, a small head, and a large beak that attached to a large belly. Talou picked up three large cloth bags and brought them outside, where he unrolled several straw mats and dumped onto them the contents of one bag. Hundreds of small sculptures and scores of masks lay scattered about like firewood. "Lobi and Gurunsi wood," Talou explained. "Next week I'll go and buy more."

Diop knelt. "As always, it's of varied quality." He picked up a small statuette of a girl—long legs, round face, thin arms and torso, and eyes shaped like cowrie shells. "For such a small piece," he said to me, "this is heavy—ironwood." He handed it to me. "That's what the Lobi use to carve these pieces." He examined several other statuettes. "What's in the other bags?"

"More Lobi and Gurunsi," Talou said.

Without examining the contents of the other bags, Diop agreed to buy all three. He also bought the four-foot hornbill. "Talou and I have been doing business for many years," he said to me. "Between us, trust is very important."

"I can see," I said.

"There's a good wholesale market for Lobi and Gurunsi wood," Diop remarked. "I should be able to ship much of it to France, and perhaps to America. One day, a tourist will buy the hornbill."

Talou loaded the art onto a cart and accompanied us back to the truck. Diop carefully loaded the hornbill, now covered by a burlap sack, into the carrier of the truck. I helped him position the three heavy sacks of Lobi and Gurunsi wood against the hornbill to cushion it.

We then went to the bar to greet Gregoire, who by now had consumed five one-liter bottles of beer. The customs officer was jovial but not drunk. He bought everyone soft drinks and invited us to sit down. "Diop," he said, "should I order several roasted chickens?"

"No, no, Gregoire. Thank you, but we need to head back."

"I understand. May God protect you on your trip."

We drove east toward the escarpment, our truck a tiny cricket amid the tall grasses. We could feel the sun's warmth on our backs. A hot breeze whipped through the open windows, carrying with it the smell of burning brush. Ahead the road snaked up toward the dusty plateau. I had learned a great deal from Diop, and yet he hadn't once lectured me about African art; he had simply invited me to share his life—if only for a little while. In Africa you learn by looking and doing. Outside of the schools, there are no textbooks, no standardized instruction, and no examinations. Fishermen take their sons out on the river to observe as they throw their nets and steer their dugouts. Carvers allow their apprentices to watch as they craft statues and masks. Weavers like Amadu ask their students to watch them work their looms. In Africa, much was learned through apprenticeship. I was an apprentice to two masters, Amadu and Diop. At that moment

I was certain that I would know Diop for many years to come. One day we'd do business together. In my mind's eye, I saw myself greeting Diop at Kennedy Airport and showing him the considerable sights of New York City. The truck's screeching brakes brought me back to the present; we had reached Torodi's customs barrier.

A short, thin customs officer stood guard. He had a carefully manicured mustache and held a cigarette between his lips. He walked up and stopped just outside of Diop's window.

"Can I see your papers, Monsieur?"

Diop got his papers from the glove compartment and gave them to the man. "Where's Idrissa?" Diop asked. "I saw him this morning."

"He went home at noon; I'm in charge now," the officer stated. He looked into the truck's carrier. "What are you bringing into Niger?"

"We have a load of art," Diop said calmly.

"Do you have a license to import art into Niger?"

"Of course, officer," Diop said. "Can I bring it into your office?"

The man took a puff on his cigarette. "Good idea."

They disappeared into the mud-brick office. After several minutes, I started to fret. What if this seemingly difficult man made trouble for Diop? My concerns were misplaced, it turned out. A moment later Diop and a now smiling officer returned. He raised the barrier and we proceeded on to Niamey, Diop's margin of profit having been unexpectedly though not significantly reduced.

TWENTY-NINE

After spending a month with Diop, I returned to Amadu's compound in Tillaberi. The season had changed: I found deep blue skies, high cirrus clouds, dry air, warm breezy days, and cool, star-filled nights. In the cool season fresh vegetables and fruit filled the market stalls. Every morning, Fulan brought milk to town. The increased water flow in the Niger meant that fishermen regularly brought to the river's edge a large and varied supply of fresh fish. Amid this relative bounty, though, some people suffered. The cool, dry air aggravated the rheumatism of old people like Amadu. Parched conditions compelled them to rub their bodies with oils and pomades. Some people had deep fissures in their heels, making it painful to walk. But these conditions did not sap the energy of the ever-active Amadu. As always, he received me with great warmth and excitement.

"My son, God has brought you back to me. I have much to tell, and even more to show you." He smiled with pride and pointed to his loom. He had made considerable progress on the commissioned wedding blanket. His son, Seyni, had gone to stay with relatives in Ouallam, but would return in perhaps a week.

After the frenetic pace of Niamey, I welcomed the relative peace and tranquility of Amadu's dune-top compound. The bush's slow pace, though, sometimes gave one too much time for contemplation. In Niamey, I had been too busy to think very much about Zeinabou. There, I spent long days at the art stall, observing sales, meeting suppliers, and watching people. The considerable energy of the market made silent reflection nearly impossible. In the evenings I returned to Diop's compound and ate sumptuous Senegalese meals. After dinner, friends would drop by. By ten o'clock I'd haul my exhausted body to bed, where I slept peacefully among the masks and statues.

Diop had taught me a great deal about African art. By handling so many pieces and by listening to Diop as he talked about the objects, I learned how to assess a mask's artistic value. Through Diop, I befriended African suppliers and European wholesalers. Diop even showed me how to pack a container. By accompanying Diop to Burkina Faso and to Nigeria, I learned how to talk to carvers as well as to the traders who wholesaled African art. In truth, I envied the full and satisfying life that Diop led. I wondered if my life would ever turn out so well. At the time, I had serious doubts. Would I ever resolve my muddied relationship with Zeinabou? If I did find her, should I offer to marry her and be a real father to my son? But I must confess that these thoughts seemed superfluous: I had no idea whether I'd ever see Zeinabou again. For now I would weave by day, write by night, and try not to think too much about Zeinabou and Ibrahim.

That night Amadu called me into his hut to throw cowrie shells. The inside of the hut glowed in the dull lantern light; the smell of kerosene permeated the air. Amadu sat on a straw mat close to the hut's center pole. A red fez covered his small shaved head. He had wrapped a striped cotton blanket around his torso to protect his old bones from the chill of night air.

"Sit, my son," he said. "It's time to prepare you for the future. We must see the paths ahead so that you'll be prepared." He opened his pouch of shells and dumped them on the smooth sand in front of him. He looked up at me. "Have you been throwing your shells, David?"

"Not so much, Baba," I replied. "When I throw them too much," I admitted, "I get headaches."

"That's a good sign, my son. That's what happens when you throw the shells. It's the spirit Wambata. She's the one who gives you headaches."

Quite frankly, I had trouble believing in Wambata, let alone her capacity to give me headaches. "I also have trouble reading my own future," I told him.

"That's always the case," Amadu said. "It took me many years to read my own path. In time, you'll be able to do it. For now you should practice on other people."

"It's not so easy. People see a white man and doubt me."

"You'll find a way, my son. That's how the shells work. Let them guide you."

At that moment I wondered if I'd ever understand Amadu's logic. His way of thinking was so alien—no instruction, no rules. I also had trouble with the idea of letting the shells take control of my destiny. When I had voiced these doubts in the past, Amadu had dismissed them with a warm laugh. Perhaps I was now ready to try Amadu's way and let the forces of the world work their magic. "Okay, Baba. I'll try to be patient and respectful."

Amadu picked up eleven shells and cupped them in his open hands. He recited an incantation and spit on them. He looked at me, lowered his head toward the sand, and threw the shells. "Yes," he responded to an inaudible voice. "I agree. Yes." He again looked at me. "There are two paths that you will soon take. There's the path of cloth, which will bring you much joy and some renown. And then there's the path of wood. You know a man who has great knowledge. You will know him for many years to come. He's a big man with a pure heart. Listen to what he says. When he asks you do to do something, make sure to do it. If you follow this man's path, you will find money."

The reading impressed me greatly. Amadu had never met Diop, and I had never talked to him about the art trader. What's more, Amadu had zeroed in on Diop's defining characteristics. How could this be? I looked at the cowries lying on the sand and pondered my next question. "Can I find happiness through wood?" I asked.

Amadu threw the cowries again and examined the positions. "It is clear that one day you will carry the burden of wood. You will talk about it to many people. You will buy it and sell it. It is not clear how wood will bring you happiness. It will comfort but also trouble you." He pointed to several shells that formed a straight line on the sand. "That," he said, "is your other path—the path of cloth. Your weaving here in Tillaberi is only a beginning, my son. When you return to America, you will no longer weave, but you will find much cloth and keep it in your compound. It will not bring you money, and you will not buy or sell it. But you will talk a great deal about it, and your words will be filled with knowledge and wisdom. This," he said, wagging his finger at the line, "will bring to you honor and respect."

Amadu's reading flooded my mind with thoughts about the burdens of life. It was true that the statues in Diop's warehouse had comforted me. I even felt that they had expelled Zeinabou from the world of my dreams, enabling me to sleep soundly. But would she return one day to haunt me? Besides, comfort did not equal happiness. I wanted more than comfort in my life. I needed love but didn't know how or with whom I might find it. I knew one thing for certain: I would never be able to love a woman until I had resolved my relationship with Zeinabou. I thought about the European men who had left their African wives and children. How could they live with themselves? Sadly, I realized that I hadn't been much better. Had I not abandoned Zeinabou and Ibrahim? Even so, my flight had exacted a heavy psychological price, for I had always felt incomplete. Although the monthly financial contributions had helped my African "family," I knew from my own life that money was no substitute for the presence of a father.

During our brief time together, my father, who was a salesman, tried to pay a great deal of attention to me. He'd regularly take me to baseball games—the Phillies—at Connie Mack Stadium. He taught me how to throw a football and showed me how to build model airplanes and boats. Sunday mornings he'd take me to the neighborhood delicatessen and proudly introduce me to his cronies. "So you're David," they would say. "Your pop has told us so much about you. He's so proud of you. He says you're real smart and that you're a real good baseball player." I remembered how good it felt to be with my dad on those mornings. When he died, everything changed. Even though my mother, a bookkeeper, worked long hours, she always made time to help me with my homework. She remained uninterested in other men, though, and never remarried. How I had wished for someone in the household to teach me more about baseball, football, and model planes. I never stopped missing my dad. If I did, indeed, have a son, I didn't want him to suffer the same fate. But life rarely presents simple solutions to complex problems. Fate had ironically tied my hands. I couldn't find Zeinabou and didn't even know if Ibrahim was of my own flesh and blood.

Lack of resolution had always made a mess of my life. In graduate school, several women had been attracted to me. A few of them wanted long-term relationships. One wanted to get married. Just before I returned to Niger to begin my research, I broke off a relationship with a beautiful and sympathetic woman, an attorney, who loved me very much. Believe me, I wanted to love her, but I couldn't express my feelings for her. There were so many times that I wanted to tell her about Zeinabou and Ibrahim. Each time, I couldn't bring myself to broach the subject. I realized then that if I wanted to have a full life, I'd have to find Zeinabou and come to terms with the emotional turbulence that had engulfed my life.

"What do the shells say of my search for my wife and son?" I asked Amadu.

He threw the cowries once again and pointed to a shell that had wedged itself laterally in the sand, a sign that my search had not progressed. "Have you been eating the tree bark powder that I gave you?"

Each time I prepared the infusion, I had disturbing dreams about Zeinabou, my son, and my father. In Niamey I felt awkward about drinking a pagan potion in the presence of Diop, a devout Muslim. "Not since I left, Baba," I answered.

Amadu spat tobacco onto the sand. "The shells don't lie. If you want to find your wife," he said, "you must drink the infusion every day. Do you understand me, my son?"

"I do."

"When the spirits tell you to do something," he insisted, "you must simply do it. Don't think about it. Just do what they say." He spat more tobacco on the sand. "Otherwise, my son," he said gravely, "you walk a path of peril. This is no game." Amadu gathered his shells and put them into his cloth satchel. "The reading is over," he said in an abrupt fashion. Then he yawned. "It's time for sleep."

Because I was wide awake, I got up and went out into the compound. I walked over to the compound's low millet-stalk fence and looked out at a bush bathed in bright moonlight. In the distance the smooth top of a sandstone butte lined the horizon. Firelight flickered at the butte's base. Trees dotted the landscape like shadowy ghosts. A donkey brayed and a breeze rustled the waxy leaves of nearby acacias. Even though the full moon had reduced the visibility of the stars that night, I could still follow the arch of the Milky Way, which divided the night sky into two halves. Bearing witness to such vastness always humbled me. How could I divest myself of my arrogance, my hubris? Who was I to ignore the sage advice of a wise man like Amadu? Did I really think that I could control my life's destiny? A shower of shooting stars streaked across the sky.

THIRTY

The next morning I told Amadu that I was ready to start my second blanket.

"You are ready, then, to have your own weaving tools," the old man replied. He went into his hut and returned with a large cloth sack and emptied its contents on the sand. There were four upright poles and a breast beam for the loom superstructure, a heddle pulley, a main heddle, a beater, and two pattern heddles that controlled the weave of warp and weft. "When you're finished with a day's work," Amadu said, looking at the disarray of loom parts, "you can pack up your loom and store it away with your unfinished cloth. When you travel," he said, "take your loom—even to America." Fifty feet away there lay a large gray stone, perhaps three feet in diameter. "That is your own dragstone. Even when you return to America, no one here will use it. It's a big one so you'll have good tension on your warp threads."

"Thank you, Baba," I said, enormously pleased by this development. Previously I had worked on someone else's loom.

"Let's assemble your loom," Amadu suggested. He showed me how to connect the upright poles to the horizontal poles that controlled the path of the weaving thread. He attached the heddles and the heddle pulley, and together we tied white warp threads to my dragstone.

"It's pretty simple, isn't it?" I observed, as we stood next to the large stone.

"Simplicity is good," Amadu said, "in both loom and pattern."

I had a fairly good eye for pattern, having already learned how to introduce simple checkerboard patterns by alternating colored threads to make both warp and weft stripes in cloth strips. "But there are many blankets," I countered, "that have complicated designs."

Amadu nodded. "That's true." He scratched his white beard. "And yet when you mature as a weaver, you see that beauty lies in simple lines." He walked over to a straw mat that lay in the shade of a hut. "Sit down, David. We must talk of weaving."

I already knew that Amadu's family had been weaving blankets for as long as anyone could remember. I also recognized that Amadu's divinatory skills, which had been passed down through the generations, were the exception rather than the rule, for Songhay weavers. What more might the old man teach me?

"Weaving," Amadu began, "is more than thread, loom, and design. It's a tradition that is older than even the Songhay. Weaving came to us from the north—beyond the Sahara. The people of the past brought us looms, wool, and patterns. Since the weaving came here, we've made new patterns. The checkerboard that you've learned is very powerful." He went on to explain how the patterns found in blankets—checkerboards, the shadow-and-light motif—referred to the relation of heaven and earth, night and day, dirt and water, men and women, life and death. "The squares and lines on the blanket are magical," Amadu said reverentially. "When we weave, we copy the world."

"Does that mean that blankets are like magic?"

The old man laughed. "Who have you been talking to?" he asked rhetorically. "Of course they are magic, but not many people know it. When we copy the world, we try to control it—the better the copy, the better the control."

Just then Amadu's son, Seyni, who had been visiting relatives in Ouallam, entered the compound. He looked at Amadu and me and scowled.

"Welcome, my son," Amada chanted.

Seyni mumbled a response, obviously disturbed about something. He walked over to my loom, examined it, and turned toward us. "Is that your loom?" he asked me.

"Yes, it is," I said with a small measure of pride.

"I see," he said, and he abruptly turned away and entered his mother's hut.

"What's wrong with him?" I asked Amadu.

Amadu hunched his shoulders.

A few moments later, Seyni came out and waved at us. "David," he said curtly, "would you come here?"

I excused myself and went over to the hut. Inside I found Seyni seated on his mother's bed, which had been fashioned from sticks. He wore a white T-shirt and a faded pair of jeans that he had found in the Tillaberi market. A cool silence settled in between us.

"Welcome back, Seyni," I said, trying to begin a conversation.

Seyni didn't respond.

"What's going on?" I asked.

"I told my relatives in Ouallam that a white man had come to sit with my father and learn to weave. That angered them. They said that you are stealing our heritage. They said that I shouldn't trust you. I told them that you were a good man and that my father liked you. I told them that you were American and that Americans are different. They said white people are infidels who can't be trusted. I didn't know what to think." Seyni paused a moment and leaned forward.

"Then I return home and what do I find? I find that Baba has given you a loom and a dragstone. And that he has told you some of our secrets."

"That's true," I admitted, thinking that an honest response might clear the air.

"Then it's true. You're stealing my heritage."

"No I'm not," I responded in an even tone. "I'm learning about weaving so I can describe your gift to many, many people. I'm like a griot. I want to carry the message of weaving to America."

"These are lies! Now I know that you will betray us. You will profit from our weaving and we'll see nothing of it. That's what the white people did to us in the past."

"It's true that white people betrayed you in the past. But they had no respect for the Songhay path."

"And you do?"

At that point I knew that I could not demonstrate my trustworthiness through words. Why should Seyni or any other Songhay person trust me? I wondered why Amadu had been willing to take me in as an apprentice and teach me how to weave and how to read shells. Like Seyni, I didn't know what to think. "I don't want to be a weaver like you," I said after a few tense moments. "And I don't want to steal your heritage. You can have my loom and dragstone."

"I don't want them," Seyni declared. "What I want is for you to leave. Baba will understand."

Saying nothing more, I left the hut and returned to the mat where Amadu sat peacefully as he chewed kola. I sat down next to the old man.

"Baba," I said, "Seyni is unhappy. He thinks I'm stealing his heritage. He's angry that you gave me a loom and a dragstone. He doesn't want you to talk to me about the weaving tradition."

"My son is young and has a quick temper," Amadu observed.

"He wants me to leave."

"What has happened to that boy's mind? He was okay when you were here before."

"He says that his relatives in Ouallam warned him about people like me."

"Those are his mother's people—all hotheads. I myself stay away from them."

"What should I do, Baba?" I asked. "I want to learn more about weaving, and I don't want to leave."

Amadu spit out some kola and rubbed his forehead. "Maybe you should go to Niamey for awhile. You have two paths now, weaving and wood. Go to your man in Niamey and learn more about wood. Continue to drink the medicine I gave you. Look for your wife and son. Your loom, unfinished blanket, and dragstone will be here.

Come back when you are ready. By then," he concluded, "the heat in my son's head will have cooled down."

I returned to Niamey the next morning.

THIRTY-ONE

The dry, dusty winds of the Nigerien cool season soon gave way to the blazing winds of the brutal hot season. Although the dawn air remained cool and fresh, by midmorning the atmosphere felt more like the inside of a furnace—fiery and enclosed. The higher the sun rose, the more blanched the sky became. Dust hung in the air like fine mist, and trees and buildings shimmered in the torrid heat.

When I first went to Niger, I soon learned that there was no full escape from the heat's oppression. There were, in fact, only brief moments of respite—a rare cool breeze savored in the shade of large tree, a stream of cool water running over hot, gritty shoulders, an ice-cold Coca-Cola running down a parched throat. If you could think of these small pleasures, you might struggle through the day and be rewarded by the first cool breezes of dusk.

By the time the hot season reached its zenith in April, I had been in Niamey for three months. Following the sage advice of Amadu, I had resumed my apprenticeship in African art with Diop. During the days we sat at Diop's stall opposite the vegetable market. Early in the day we bought inventory, mostly silver jewelry from Tuareg smiths or from local suppliers. Later in the morning we studied books on African art. Occasionally, we talked to tourists. At midday we returned to Diop's compound to eat lunch and take a siesta. Late afternoons we were back at Diop's stall, where we talked to potential buyers. In the evenings Diop and I returned home to consume delicious Senegalese dinners and engage in animated conversations with friends. Since it was far too stifling to sleep in the storeroom, I brought my bed into the courtyard and slept—quite soundly—under the stars.

This satisfying routine conveniently enabled me to ignore my troubles. What's more, I learned a great deal from Diop and his friends. My field notes now described in great detail how traders found African art, both authentic and reproduced, and how they shipped and marketed it to international wholesalers. In fact, life in Niamey had captivated me to such a degree that I hadn't thought very much about Zeinabou and Ibrahim, let alone the falling out with Seyni that had exiled me from Tillaberi.

One morning Diop brought to my outdoor bedside a steaming cup of coffee. He opened a folding chair and sat down. "David," he said softly. "Here's some coffee."

I opened my eyes to see an immense form seated on a chair near my cot. "Wha?"

I sat up and struggled to free myself from mosquito netting that had been securely tucked under the mattress. Free at last, I sat on the bed's edge, sipped the coffee, and tried to wake up. I looked at my watch. "I've been sleeping for ten hours," I yawned. "I can't remember when I've slept so well."

Diop stared at me. "It's time," he said nonchalantly and paused a moment. "It's time for you to look for your wife and child."

Diop's thunderbolt immediately erased my sleepiness. "I'm not going to find them, Diop."

"I've heard they're in town," Diop announced.

"What?"

"Since you've been here, I've been making inquiries," Diop said. "Finally, I have some news. A little boy, who could be Ibrahim, lives in a small compound adjoining a bar on the other side of the river— not far from the circle in the road. The bar there is run by a Fulan woman."

That news jolted me into action. In no time at all I found myself seated on Diop's rusty motorbike, maneuvering my way through the Niamey traffic. The mix of truck exhaust and wood smoke made the city air noxious. My eyes burned and my lungs ached. In my haste to escape the city, I almost ran into a wood-burdened donkey mesmerized by a red traffic light. Two lepers, dressed in tattered robes, hobbled over to me.

"White man," they said. "Give us alms. We are God's children." They waved their stump hands in my face to make their point. After I gave each of them a contribution, they moved on to the next patron. Meanwhile the light turned green, and I puttered toward the John F.

Kennedy Bridge, which as usual was clogged with traffic—trucks, cars, motorbikes, camels, donkeys, and pedestrians. At least on the other side of the river the traffic would subside a bit. I crossed the bridge quickly and headed west toward my destination, wondering if I would at last see Zeinabou and meet Ibrahim. What would I say to her? What if she refused to talk to me? What if she refused to let me see or talk to Ibrahim? No matter how hard I tried to think about what to do, nothing came to mind. I had waited years for this moment to happen, but now that it was perhaps upon me, my mind was empty, my plan of action nonexistent. The shrill sound of a whistle broke my concentration. Standing next to his motorcycle, a policeman waved me over to the side of the road. In my haste, I had left Diop's without taking my driver's license, passport, or Diop's motorbike registration papers. I made my way to the makeshift police stop and tried to gather my cool.

"Good morning, sir," the policeman said. He was a tall, thin man dressed in a crisp khaki uniform. A motorcycle helmet framed his face. "Can I see your papers?"

I had to think quickly. If the encounter with the policeman did not go well, which was a distinct possibility, I'd have to spend the rest of the morning, perhaps the whole day, paying fines and filling out forms. I decided to talk to the man in Songhay.

"How is your morning?" I asked. "And how is the health of your wife, your children, and the people of your compound?" We exchanged greetings for several moments.

"Your Songhay is good," the policeman commented. "It's good that you speak our language. It shows respect."

I briefly told the policeman about my years in Tera and Tillaberi and about my current project. I mentioned Amadu, whose name was widely known in western Niger. I also spoke to the policeman about Diop. "This is his motorbike. He loaned it to me so I could do an errand in this neighborhood."

"I can see you are a good man," the policeman said. "And I'm impressed with your Songhay." He paused a moment. "But I need to see your papers."

"I forgot to bring them."

"You have no identification or registration papers?"

"I'm afraid I don't."

"Ah, Monsieur David, this is a serious situation. I could put you in jail. Perhaps you are riding a stolen motorbike. At the very least, you are driving without a license and proper identification—a serious offense, my friend."

I knew that I had to let the policeman have his moment and keep my cool. "I'd be happy to take you to Diop's. He can identify the motorbike, and I can show you my passport and my authorization to conduct research."

The policeman smiled and waved his hand back and forth. "We don't need to do that, Monsieur David. You're telling me the truth. But we need to deal with the infraction, don't we?"

"Yes, of course."

"You know, Monsieur David, life has become difficult in Niger . . ."

I knew where the conversation was going and remained a captive listener.

" . . . Everything is more expensive—food, rent, clothing, school fees for my children. The problem is that they don't pay us very much. We can't even count on getting paid every month. Can you imagine?"

"Sounds tough," I said.

"You bet it is. At midmonth, I'm broke. Even so, my relatives in the countryside think I'm made of money. They ask me for money to buy food. How can I refuse relatives who have nothing?"

"You can't."

"Of course I can't. I think we understand one another, don't we?"

"I think we do," I said with a smile on my face. I reached into my pocket and pulled out some money I had hastily—and fortuitously—stuffed in there before I set out. I folded the money into my palm and shook hands with the policeman—a decorous mechanism of exchange.

The policeman took his bribe and nodded. "You can go now, Monsieur David. Next time remember your papers when you leave your house."

As I rode away from the police stop, leaving in my wake a cloud of dust, I hoped that my encounter at the bar would also result in a positive outcome. In a matter of minutes, I saw the circle in the road and to the left a building in front of which tables had been set up in the shade of two tall acacias. As I drove closer, I saw a sign that read "Bar

Fofo." A smaller building, perhaps a house, had been built some one hundred meters to the left of the bar's entrance. My heart raced. Was this my moment? I took several deep breaths to calm the flutter in my stomach. I parked the motorbike in the shade near the tables and walked toward the open door. As sweat rolled down my back, my head throbbed. I clapped three times outside the door.

"Come in."

I tentatively stepped into the cool darkness. Sunlight streaming through the small square windows illuminated dust in the air. Behind the bar, which looked like it had been fashioned from cement-covered mud bricks, there stood a tall Fulan woman who was not Zeinabou. She had lustrous copper skin, an angular face, and a long, thin nose, offset by large almond eyes. I stared at her and said nothing.

"Hello Anasaara," she said in French. "Do you want something to drink?"

"Thanks," I said in Songhay. Even though it was early in the day, I felt like drinking something alcoholic. "I'll have a beer." I sat down on one of the barstools.

She smiled. "You speak Songhay? That's good." She walked over to a humming refrigerator, took out a cold Bière Niger, opened it, and poured me a glass. "What brings you here, Anasaara?"

"My name is David."

The woman smiled. "My name is Mariama," she said pleasantly. "So why have you come to this out-of-the-way bar?" she asked as she smiled at me. "There are far better bars in Niamey."

"That's right," I said, emboldened a bit by the beer, "but I heard that this one was run by a Fulan woman who had a little boy."

Mariama laughed. "Is that so?" She paused. "Well I'm the Fulan woman who runs the bar, and my son, Adam, lives next door." She rested her palms on the bar. "Did Etienne send you here?"

"No one sent me here," I answered, "and I know no one called Etienne."

"You are luckier than me," she said flatly, convinced, perhaps, of the veracity of my statement. "Five years ago he said he loved me and wanted to marry me. I got pregnant and he left. He said he'd send for me. He said that I'd like France." She put her hands on her hips. "Well, I've never seen France. And Adam, who is now five years old, has never seen his father. My son is a baturé, half white, half black. Do you know how hard it is to be a baturé in Niger? No one accepts him. The other children call him 'baturé' or 'Anasaara.' Everyone knows that his father is one of those white men who refused to be a husband or a father." The woman began to weep. "Do you know what I'm talking about, Monsieur David?"

The pressure of shame bore down on my neck and shoulders. How blind I had been! I had been so self-possessed that I had thought little about what life in Niger would be like for someone like Ibrahim. I looked up at this sad woman. "Don't cry Mariama. Don't cry," I said. "For what it's worth, I know what it's like. I lost my father when I was ten years old."

"I feel bad for you, Monsieur David." She took a deep breath. "But at least you knew your father."

"And for that I'm grateful," I said softly.

Mariama poured more beer into my glass. "What about my first question, Monsieur David." She paused a moment. "Why did you come here today?"

I decided that it would be better to reveal partial truths than to bring more pain and anger to this soulful woman. "I thought you might be a woman I knew when I lived in Niger five years ago," I explained delicately. "I heard that, like you, she had a son."

"You mean a baturé child?"

"That's right. I thought I should come by and pay my respects."

"I guess you made a mistake," she said, softly. "But I'm glad you came. You seem like a good man."

"I've made my fair share of mistakes."

"Would you like to meet Adam?" Mariama asked. "I think he'd like you."

The tightness in my shoulders eased. "Yes. Where is he?"

Mariama led me out of the bar into blinding midday light. We turned toward the small mud-brick house. A two-foot wall separated the bar and house from a small grove of acacia trees. Putting my hand flat against my brow to shield my eyes from the glare, I noticed several boys sitting in the shade amid the trees. Two donkeys stood near by. A scrawny brown dog lay on its side, panting. "Adam," Mariama chanted. "They're calling for you. They're calling for you."

Moments later, a short, copper-skinned boy with straight brown hair as coarse as steel wool came through an opening in the wall. He wore blue gym shorts and a ragged pair of tennis shoes.

"Come here, Adam," Mariama insisted. She waved.

The boy stared at me but refused to approach.

"Why don't you come closer?" I said softly in Songhay.

The boy remained rooted to his spot.

"Am I a donkey?"

The boy giggled.

"Am I a lion?"

"No!"

Adam finally approached. I held out my hand and Adam took it. He touched my skin and ran his fingers along the hair that covered my arm. He looked up at me and squinted. "Come and play with me."

"Adam, we need to eat lunch," Mariama said.

"I'm not hungry. I want him to play with me."

"Can I come back and play?" I asked.

The boy nodded.

I looked at Mariama. "Is it okay if I come back and see you both?"

"It's okay. Come anytime."

On my way back to Niamey I reflected on the irony of the encounter. How strange it had been to find a woman and young boy in virtually the same circumstances as Zeinabou and Ibrahim. In the distance I saw the motorcycle policeman again. Would this shameless man hit me up yet again? As I got closer, I heard the policeman's whistle. Once again the officer waved me over. Expecting the worst, I drove the motorbike to the shady spot where the policeman had positioned himself.

"I see that you're returning to Niamey," the policeman said amiably.

"I am," I said sullenly.

"Get off your bike," the policeman ordered. He pointed to two chairs under the tree. "Let's sit down."

A cool breeze blew in from the west. "Do you want to know more about my papers?"

"That's long forgotten," the policeman said. "Let's have some tea and you can tell me about your day."

THIRTY-TWO

Two days later I returned to the Bar Fofo to see Mariama and Adam. Again I borrowed Diop's motorbike, and remembering this time to carry the registration papers, I headed toward the setting sun. The late-afternoon light seeped into Niamey's trees, scrub bushes, and buildings, giving them a soothing glow. By now the heat had subsided and cool breezes from the west swept across the landscape. Approaching the river's edge, I saw a solitary fisherman, perched on the bow of his dugout, poling his boat upstream. Several women scrubbed pots and pans in the shallows. Overhead, a small squadron of squawking ducks flew in formation.

The evening after my first visit to the Bar Fofo, I had told Diop of my adventures and of my intention to visit Mariama and Adam again.

"Be careful, my friend," Diop advised. "You don't want to fall for this Fulan, do you?"

"Don't be ridiculous," I retorted. "I feel bad for them, that's all."

"Do you feel bad for them or for yourself?"

I smiled and nodded. "You're a wise man, Diop. You're right, of course. Like me, they're sad. Mariama was abandoned and little Adam has no father."

"Just like Zeinabou and Ibrahim," Diop observed.

"I know. I know."

"Don't use these people to avoid your responsibilities, my friend."

Despite this sensible advice, I bought Adam a book of children's stories and a soccer ball. Maybe these small tokens would lighten a bit the heavy social burdens that the little boy had already endured.

As I crossed the John F. Kennedy Bridge, the sun slipped behind the three majestic buttes that dominate Niamey's western horizon. My thoughts drifted to life's contingencies. How strange that I thought I was about to have a stressful encounter with Zeinabou, a tightly wound woman, only to happen upon Mariama, who seemed much more mellow. And it had been wonderful to meet Adam. Even so, my excitement could have been a classic example of Jean-Paul Sartre's notion of bad faith. Was my life-in-the-world simply a network of patched-together illusions about myself? That was one possibility. I also thought of Amadu's confounding logic. Every day, I had been preparing and ingesting Amadu's medicine. Perhaps the fortuitous encounter with Mariama and Adam hadn't been mere happenstance. It might have been a sign to follow one of Amadu's paths. I parked the motorbike in front of the bar, untied the package from the bike rack, slowly walked to the door, and clapped three times.

"Entrez," she said.

"It's me," I said shyly. No one else was in the bar.

"Welcome back, Monsieur David." Her eyes fixed on the package. "What have you brought?"

"A book and a soccer ball for Adam," I answered.

Mariama shook her head slowly and slapped her hand on the bar. "You *are* a good man," she said. She came around from behind the bar and, saying nothing, slipped outside. "Adam, come. Adam come," she cried.

She turned toward me. "Come outside, Monsieur David. Adam will be here right away."

The scrawny boy with coarse hair came running up to Mariama and me. Showing none of his previous hesitation, he took my hand.

"Come and play with me," he said.

"Adam, say hello to Uncle David."

"Hello, *Ton Ton* David. Come and play."

I produced the square box, wrapped in bright blue paper. "It's for you, Adam."

I handed the box to the boy.

Adam put the box on the dirt, ripped it apart, pulled out the soccer ball, and bounced it several times on the ground.

I took out the book I had brought. "I brought this for you, too. Maybe I'll read you some stories."

Ignoring the book, Adam grabbed my hand. We walked hand in hand toward a sandy expanse bordered by a line of acacias. As we played with the soccer ball, Adam screamed with delight. I showed him how to hit the ball with his head.

We played until dusk, when Mariama called us back to the bar to eat dinner. Several patrons, Nigeriens all, drank beer at an outdoor table under the trees. Adam and I sat down a few tables away from the patrons. A cool breeze rustled through the trees. In short order, Mariama brought a platter to the table. I breathed deeply to take in the pungent aroma emanating from the smaller of two white enamel bowls. Slowly, I lifted the lid. "What is it?" I asked.

"Fish stew with a spicy sauce. See how you like it," she said.

I put a plate in front of Adam and, using a large wooden spoon, served him a portion of rice from the larger bowl. I then poured some sauce onto his plate, making sure to give him several large chunks of fish. "More sauce, Adam?"

Adam nodded. "I'm hungry."

I set a place for Mariama, served her a portion, and then served myself.

"Is that all you're eating?" Mariama asked me as she sat down.

"I wanted to make sure that everyone got enough to eat."

Mariama laughed loudly. "You Americans will never understand. Here we don't have much, but when we prepare food, we always make more than we can eat. Who knows, maybe a friend or perhaps a stranger will wander by and need something to eat. Maybe a beggar will ask us for an offering. How can we refuse? And if no one eats what's left, we heat it up for breakfast in the morning."

"I know. I know," I said, remembering once again how much I admired the ways Africans could make so much from so little. "I'll serve myself more rice and more sauce."

"Don't be shy," Mariama commanded. "There's more rice and sauce in the kitchen." She looked at Adam and smiled. "You see," she said to me, "my boy has already finished one helping."

"Hey Adam, hey," I called.

The boy looked up from his plate and smiled, revealing a missing front tooth.

"Do you like Coca-Cola?"

"Yes, Uncle."

"Mariama, could you kindly bring us three Cocas and perhaps some more food?"

"I'll bring them with pleasure, Monsieur David."

As darkness fell, Mariama put some African Pop cassettes into a boom box. She brought out a Petromax Lamp, which flooded the tables with bright light. After dinner, Adam sat on my lap. I started to read. By the middle of the second story, he had fallen fast asleep.

THIRTY-THREE

Late one stifling afternoon toward the end of the hot season, I found myself in the passenger seat of the battered Peugeot 504 of Jean-Jacques Meyrac, a professor at the Tillaberi Normal School. Meyrac was a short, pudgy man with bushy black hair, a round face, and small black eyes. The state of Meyrac's car was legendary. The windows in the back couldn't be opened, a web of cracks in the windshield dangerously reduced visibility, the old tires leaked air, and the engine frequently overheated.

Meyrac, who chain-smoked Galloises, loved living in Niger as much as he adored his old car. One must confront difficulties, this professor of philosophy once told me during a drunken moment at the Giraffe Bar, in order appreciate fully the texture of a relationship. Meyrac had been teaching in Niger for seven happy years. The French government paid him well, and the Nigerien government provided him a large villa on the Normal School campus. He had a particularly skillful Togolese cook and a beautiful Songhay girlfriend.

The amplitude of the engine's drone made conversation impossible. As we chugged and sputtered northward, I looked passively at the mesmerizing landscape. The treeless red-clay plain was strewn with black rocks, and smooth sandstone ridges rose from the ground like brown skin that had been pinched. Clusters of leafless trees sprouted here and there from clay fields. Packs of vultures picked at a donkey carcass lying along the side of the road. For weeks I had resisted returning to Tillaberi to resume my apprenticeship with Amadu. Visits to Mariama and Adam had been particularly satisfying, and Diop had taught me a great deal about distinguishing fake from authentic African art. As we got closer to Tillaberi, I wondered if the passage of time had dissipated Seyni's anger. Would I be able to resume my apprenticeship? In a happy state of aimless lethargy, I had avoided these problems. Then Meyrac materialized at Diop's art stall. Seeing Meyrac jolted me from my personal diversions. Right then and there I decided that it was time to return to Tillaberi. After a brief discussion about the state of Tillaberi, Meyrac offered me a ride in his venerable car.

By the time Meyrac left me at the auto depot, the sun's descent toward the west had sapped much of its intensity. As always, Angu, the stationmaster, had positioned himself on a bench on the veranda in front of the station. Whiling away the time, he talked with several cronies. When Meyrac dropped me off, Angu turned in my direction and stood up. "Ah, Monsieur David. You've returned. Welcome."

"Thanks, Monsieur Angu."

"Are you going up to Amadu's?"

He turned toward two young boys playing in the distance. "Hey, children, hey. Come here and give us a hand."

Expecting a sweet and previously unanticipated reward in exchange for their efforts, the two boys came running and took my bags.

"Angu, it's good, as always, to see you."

Angu shook his head. "I'll never understand white people," he said. "I lived in Paris all those years, and still don't understand you."

"What do you mean?" I asked.

"Meyrac knew that you were going to Amadu's, right?"

"That's right."

"Then why in God's name did he leave you here to walk two kilometers in the heat?"

"He's a strange one, that Meyrac," I observed.

"I'll say."

"Maybe he was afraid his car would get stuck in the sand up there."

Angu shook with laughter. "Why worry about that old pot of a car. White people make me laugh, my friend."

I smiled inwardly at the profound irony of the conversation. "I guess I should begin that two-kilometer walk, right?"

"Yes, indeed, my friend. But before you return to America, you must come to visit. I miss our conversations. Come and drink beer and we'll talk about Sartre and Merleau-Ponty."

"You've got my word."

When my entourage reached Amadu's compound, the amber glow of the day's last light was angling into the huts and houses. At the compound entrance, I clapped three times. Amadu himself peered toward me and clapped his hands.

"David's come. David's come."

I paid the helpers, took my bags, and walked into the compound.

Amadu shook my hand and once again welcomed me to his home. Amadu's wives emerged from their huts and clapped their hands. "David's come," they cried. "David's come."

Seyni sat passively on the edge of a wooden bed and stared at me. Slowly, he stood up and walked toward Amadu and me. Without saying a word, he took my bag and put it in his father's hut.

Amadu invited me to sit on a mat under the tamarind tree. I told him about my adventures in Niamey. I spoke of Diop, and of looking for Zeinabou and Ibrahim but finding Mariama and Adam. I recounted what Diop had taught me about African art.

Amadu listened as he took some kola from the pocket in his tunic and, picking up a grater from the mat, scraped the nut into a pulp, which he put under his lip. "My teeth aren't strong enough to chew," he commented, smiling at me.

As night fell, a silence descended between us. These silences, which were not infrequent in Amadu's world, disturbed me. Seyni had silently taken my bag, an action that suggested a measure of hospitality, which, in turn, suggested that his anger had abated. Why not say so? Amadu had listened as I related a series of events that meant a great deal to me, but said nothing. Like most Americans, I wanted some kind of affirmation.

"I like this part of the day," Amadu said, breaking the silence. "It's between day and night. It's a place between two moments."

What on earth is he talking about? I wondered, dutifully keeping my silence.

"Yes." He spit out some kola. "That's the place where the spirits live—a place of wonder, but also of danger." He looked up at the darkening sky. "It's good that you have been eating the plants I gave you. Continue to eat them. And when you're finished, I'll give you more to take back to America."

"Thank you, Baba," I said.

"They will bring us millet and sauce soon, and Seyni will join us for dinner. Tomorrow, we will all weave together. You have much work to do on your blanket."

The next morning we woke up before dawn, drank tea, and prepared to weave. As usual, we set up our looms in the shade of the tamarind tree, arranged our beaters and pulleys, and extended our warp threads to dragstones. When the tension in the warp threads was sufficient, we sat down at our looms and began to weave, which meant that it was time for Amadu to talk.

"A long time ago," Amadu began, "three men sat down at their looms to weave. The first man said, 'Would it not be wonderful if the world was like a blanket—warp and weft combining in patterns that create beauty?' The second man said, 'That world would be wonderful. We could weave the world and there would be no conflict, no jealousies, and no betrayals.' The third and oldest weaver said, 'A blanket, my brothers, cannot change the world. It cannot rid the world of conflict, jealousies, and betrayals. We can weave the world and that act brings to it the great beauty that our patterns and colors provide. That beauty protects us, if only a little, from conflict, jealousy, and betrayal.' 'But how can we be sure that our threads will protect people?' the first weaver wondered. 'Why weave, if weaving cannot set the world straight?' the second weaver asked. 'We weave,' the third weaver said, 'because it was the passion of our ancestors. It is also our passion. We must make sure that that passion, which connects past and present, is woven into our textiles. It's the passion that protects, that makes the world a little bit more like a blanket.' 'But we weave and weave,' the first weaver argued, 'and it makes no difference in the world.' 'How do we live in the world?' the second weaver asked. 'With patience,' the third weaver said. 'If you are patient and vigilant, you will find what you're looking for. Your path will open. You will bring beauty to the world.'"

"Baba," said Seyni, "do we have to listen to these fables while we weave? How many times have I heard that story?"

"You cannot hear it too many times," Amadu stated. "One day you will recount it to your sons, and your sons to their sons. That is our way, Seyni. Life is patience."

I marveled at the indirect, powerful way Amadu communicated. The story, of course, had many meanings, some quite practical, some quite philosophical. After hearing Amadu's story, I knew I would find Zeinabou before I returned to the United States. Somehow, some way, I would see her and try to set things straight between us. As I combined warp and weft on my loom under the tamarind tree, I tried to weave my own life into a pattern. I could see how certain threads intersected, but as hard as I tried, I still couldn't fathom a pattern.

Like the weavers of the past, I, too, would have to weave a strong thread of patience into my life.

THIRTY-FOUR

After the peace, quiet, and productivity of the countryside, I found Niamey's dirt, dust, and noise cumbersome, if not irritating. It was August, the peak of the Nigerien rainy season. The intense, dry heat of May and June had been replaced by a steamy humidity brought on by frequent downpours, especially in the late afternoon and evening. Sprouting from what had been brown, lifeless plains, grasses now gave the countryside a vibrant green hue. Millet grew tall and golden in the fields, and sunlight sparkled in rain-cleansed air. That year the downpours had been particularly heavy, washing away several mud-brick houses. Large puddles of muddy water colonized many of Niamey's dirt streets and pathways.

In two weeks' time I would return to America—to New Haven— to take up my duties as a teaching assistant and write a dissertation. I hoped it would take me no longer than eighteen months more to earn my doctorate. Then I could look for a job. Having only two weeks to put my affairs in order, I had little time to ponder these future possibilities. After all, I had to reconfirm my airline reservations, write a research report for the Fulbright-Hays people, present a lecture on my work at the American Cultural Center, and buy parting gifts for my many friends. I also wanted to spend time with Diop and visit my new friends Mariama and Adam. Attention to these diverting details, of course, enabled me to partially repress an ever-increasing anxiety about finding Zeinabou and Ibrahim.

Relishing my descent into detail, I finalized the flight to America, wrote the research report to the Fulbright-Hays Commission, and gave a well-received lecture at the American Cultural Center. The talk focused on Nigerien weaving traditions. The audience consisted of Nigerien professors and students with a smattering of Americans. After the lecture, the Nigeriens peppered me with questions ranging from the history of weaving to the symbolic meanings of patterns.

One week before my departure, Diop proposed to make me a business partner. He would ship art to me in America, and I would wholesale it to gallery owners. I tried to explain that I would have little time to devote to business matters. Ignoring my protests, Diop told me that I would receive a shipment of trade beads along with a list of potential clients. "You'll get it in two months," Diop said.

"But I can't do it," I protested. "I'll be too busy."

"You'll find a way. And from what I hear, you'll need the extra money. Think of it as a part-time job."

I realized that resistance, as Americans would one day be fond of saying, was futile. "One way or another something will happen."

That morning both suppliers and clients were in short supply at Diop's shop. Humidity from an overnight downpour had made the air thick. The absence of even a light breeze made it uncomfortable.

"It's a bad time for business," Diop observed. "The rains make the roads impassable. Suppliers can't transport their pieces. As for tourists, they usually come in December, when it's cool and dry. This time is good for the millet, but bad for everyone else. It's the time for malaria: more puddles, more mosquitoes."

"I know. It's a bad time for malaria. But the worst of it is during the harvest in October. That's why it is called *hemar'izo*, the child of the harvest."

Diop listened passively. "Everything is so slow," he observed, "even our conversation." He frowned at me. "What are you doing here? Why not look for your wife and son?"

I looked at the ground. "I don't know if I'll ever find them," I lamented. "I just don't have it in me to look anymore. I'd rather spend my last days here with you and Mariama and Adam."

Good friend that he was, Diop would not let the matter go. "If you leave here without knowing the truth about Zeinabou, how can you go on?"

"I'll find a way," I said, now looking at my good friend. "I'm beginning to understand Amadu's way of looking at the world. We can control some parts of our lives, it's true. But there's so much we can't control. I'll simply let the world weave its own patterns. If I don't see Zeinabou on this trip, perhaps I'll find her the next time I come. I may never see her again. I accept these possibilities."

"But what will you do about your obligations?"

"I will honor them as best I can," I said solemnly. At that, I stood up. "Can I borrow your motorbike?"

"Are you going to see that woman and her son?"

"Yes."

"Be careful, my friend."

"Don't worry, Diop. They're good friends and that is all."

By midmorning I arrived at the Fofo Bar, which was still closed. The sun had evaporated much of the morning's humidity, but the evening rainwater had sunk deeply into the sandy ground, which remained heavy and damp.

The door to Mariama's house had been left ajar: bright light opening to a sliver of obscurity. Bearing my customary package of gifts for Adam, I walked toward the house. When I heard the murmur of conversation, I clapped three times.

"Come in," Mariama said.

I popped my head inside. The room was cool, but dank. The smell of mildew permeated the space. "How is your morning?"

Mariama and a young girl, tall and thin and perhaps ten years old, sat in the corner of the room on the end of a stick bed. Three shafts of light from open windows cut through the darkness, revealing two walls covered with striped blankets, several cast-iron pots on the floor, and an armoire, painted red and yellow, filled with brightly patterned enamel bowls and plates. Shielded by a baby blue canopy and dressed with striped blankets, a bed stood at the other end of the room. They both looked at me. "Wait one minute, Monsieur David," she said. She turned back to the girl. "Make sure to get a good cut of meat, and bring carrots, onions, and dried tomatoes," she said in Songhay. "And go to the boutique and buy one can of coffee and two measures of green tea."

"Yes, Mariama," the girl said. "Is there anything else?"

"Don't forget some hard candy for Adam."

Without saying another word, the girl slipped out into the brightness.

Mariama turned toward me. "Come and sit down, Monsieur David." She looked at the package. "You're going to spoil the boy."

"I just want him to have a few things. Where is he?"

"He's playing with his friends," she answered. "What did you bring him this time?"

I opened the package and took out several T-shirts, two pairs of trousers, a pair of sandals, three tablets of unlined paper, and a package of crayons. I gave Mariama some Nivaquine tablets. "Malaria season is coming. You both should take these every day to avoid getting sick."

"Thank you, Monsieur David. You're really like an older brother to me. And Adam loves his uncle very much."

Being an only child, I had never had a brother, let alone a sister. I did have aunts and uncles, but saw them infrequently—they lived far away and visited Philadelphia only one or two times a year. Accordingly, giving gifts to Mariama and Adam brought me great pleasure.

"Mariama," I said, "I need to tell you something before I leave."

"I'm listening."

"When I return to America, I will not forget you. I want you to give me your post office box number so I can send money to you and Adam. I want you to have the medicine and clothes you need. I'd like for Adam to go to a good school—a private school. I want to pay for these things."

"We thank God for bringing you into our lives. We thank God," Mariama exclaimed. "We'll never forget you." She took hold of my hand and began to cry.

I sat silently next to her, savoring a blissful moment. At that moment I did not know if I'd ever again see Mariama and Adam, but felt that we would be connected, however distantly, for many years to come. "Mariama," I said softly, "please give me your post office box number."

She found a notebook, ripped out a page, and wrote the number. "Don't lose it."

"I'm not going to lose it," I said. "Give me another piece of paper. I'll give you my address."

"You'll hear from us," Mariama said.

I stood up. "I should go."

"But you haven't seen Adam yet!"

"I know. I know." I didn't want to explain how difficult it would be to say goodbye to the little boy. "Send me photos of him. I want to see him grow up."

Mariama wiped tears from her eyes. "May God protect you, David."

I reproached myself as I crossed the John F. Kennedy Bridge on my way back to Niamey. Although I had visited Mariama and Adam at least five times, I had not yet brought Adam's mother a personal gift. How could I have been so thoughtless! Right then and there, I decided to buy her some fine cloth imported from Europe. There was a cloth shop just opposite the central market. Although I had never shopped there, I had many times walked by the boutique's window and noticed displays of fine lace and damask cloth.

When I parked Diop's motorbike in front of the cloth shop, a young boy, his right leg twisted by polio, hobbled his way to my side. Leaning on his one and only crutch, he touched my hand. "You need a guardian, Monsieur. I'll keep people away from your moto."

I agreed. "I shouldn't be too long," I said.

The boy smiled. "Your moto is in good hands."

I walked through the door and had a surreal vision: it was Zeinabou standing behind the counter staring at me. Our eyes locked. An interminable silence settled between us. Who would break it? What would we talk about?

Looking elegantly cool and slim in a white-on-white damask outfit with gold embroidery that swirled around the garment's neck, Zeinabou sat down on her chair. "I wondered whether our paths would cross again," she said.

"I've been here almost a year," I said, a bit breathlessly. "I didn't know where to find you. My letters and money orders were returned to me marked: 'Not at this address.' I looked for you for a long time."

"Looks like your search is over," she said.

"Funny, but I had given up. I came here only to buy a going away gift. I go back to America next week."

"I hope you have a safe journey," she said passively.

"Why didn't you write? Why didn't you send me a forwarding address?"

Zeinabou's beauty hadn't faded with time. The smooth skin of her shapely face glowed in the light. Her eyes sparkled. "At first, your money helped Ibrahim and me. Later, we didn't need your help."

"How long have you worked here?" I asked.

"I own this shop," she said with pride.

Zeinabou's coolness made me timid. How resourceful she had been. She had taken a small amount of money and had established a successful business. "It looks like business is good."

"I thank God," she said. "Why don't you come in and look around? I have some fine cloth."

I walked over to a display of white-on-white damask like she was wearing and touched the fabric. "I want to buy something for Madame Diop," I stated, concealing the identity of the gift's intended recipient. "I'll buy three meters."

Zeinabou joined me at the display. "This cloth will make Madame Diop very happy." She cut three meters of cloth from the bolt and wrapped the cloth in gold gift paper. "That will be four thousand francs."

After paying her, I could contain myself no longer. "What about Ibrahim?" I asked almost in a whisper.

Zeinabou smiled. "He is very tall for his age—and very good looking."

"Is he in Niamey?" I asked, hoping beyond hope for an invitation to see the boy.

"No. He's with my mother's people. It's easier to be a mixed child in the country."

My chin dropped toward my chest. "I see."

Zeinabou examined some lace cloth and then looked at me. "You had a chance, but you abandoned us. You thought I lied about Ibrahim. You thought someone else was the father."

"Yes," I said. "I was young and I had doubts."

"I have something to show you," she said. She led me to the counter. "Stay there." She went behind the counter and produced an envelope, from which she took out a photograph of Ibrahim. "Look at my boy."

I saw a tall, thin, copper-skinned boy who was unmistakably my son—the same eyes, the same chin, and the same nose! "He looks like me," I said with no small measure of pride.

"Yes, he does. You helped to produce him, but he's never had a father. Ibrahim has a difficult life ahead of him. I won't allow you to make it even more confusing. Can you understand that?"

What could I say? The fact of biological paternity would not magically make me Ibrahim's father. I also realized that although my financial contributions counted for something, money gave me no rights to the boy. "I understand," I said. "But I still want to do something for him."

"We don't want your money," Zeinabou insisted.

Blood rushed to my face. "He's my son! I can't put him out of my mind."

Zeinabou arched her back, but did not object to my statement. "There's nothing you can do."

For one year I had tried to project the many twists and turns that this conversation might take. In the end, I knew what to say. "I want Ibrahim to have a good education."

"I can give him what he needs," Zeinabou said flatly.

"I don't doubt that for a moment. But if life is going to be hard for him, I want him to be well prepared."

Zeinabou nodded cautiously.

"I want to open a bank account for his education. I'll send money to it every month. That way, he can go to private school. Maybe one day he could use the money to study at a university in Europe."

"And what do you want?" Zeinabou asked skeptically.

"Ibrahim doesn't have to know about me. All you need to do is send me a letter and a picture once a year."

"That's it. No other demands?"

"I've told you what I want. As long as I get letters and pictures, I'll send money to the account."

She shrugged and extended her hand. "I give you my word."

Just then several women entered the store, a good time for me to gracefully take my leave. Outside, I stole one last look at Zeinabou, who was holding up some cloth for one of the customers. Wondering if I'd ever meet Ibrahim, I felt a tug on my sleeve.

"You see Monsieur," said the young boy who had protected Diop's motorbike from thieves, "your moto is safe."

"Indeed it is," I said with a sense of satisfaction. "You've done well." I gave the boy three hundred francs, about ten times the going rate for such service, and drove back to Diop's.

NEW YORK 1998

The sizzle of dough slipping into hot oil broke the intensity that my story had brought into the gallery. Soon the smell of beignets wafted into the room. By now, we had long since finished our third glass of tea, and Elli, who had heard my story many times, had gone to the gallery's back room—and kitchen—to brew more tea and prepare chenchena, fried bean cakes, a food usually consumed with tea late in the Nigerien afternoon.

Mamadou stretched his long legs. "Africa spoiled you, David," he said. "You eat these wonderful sauces, drink strong green tea, and in the afternoon you eat bean cakes."

"Elli made them for you," I said. "She makes a good chenchena, my friend. In Niger I ate them every afternoon with hot sauce. Here, we have to buy our hot sauce at a West Indian grocery store." I stood up, stretched, and walked to the back room to bring in the tea, chenchena, and hot sauce. Elli followed me to the low table and sat down.

"I've been listening so much to David's story," Mamadou said, looking at Elli, "that I haven't noticed if anyone has come into the gallery."

Elli shrugged. "Not today. During the week most days are slow."

"That's difficult."

"It's not so bad," Elli said. "We've got clients. We send them photos and ship them pieces on advisement. They like what we have and have confidence in us. We also go to shows, and that works out well."

Smiling at Elli, Mamadou reached out to touch her hand lightly. "Next time we come here, we'll have to hear your story."

Elli smiled. "If you want to hear that one, be prepared to stay until midnight."

Everyone laughed.

As I sipped my tea, Mamadou turned to me. "So tell me, David, did Zeinabou send you letters and photos every year?"

"She kept her word and I kept mine. Every year I got a letter and a photo. That way, I watched Ibrahim grow up. He did quite well at school and grew tall like his papa. When he was twelve, Zeinabou enrolled him in a private middle school. He continued on to a private high school, where he got high grades and graduated near the top of his class."

"Did he go to a university?"

"He went to the Sorbonne."

"Wonderful," Mamadou said.

"They should have given him a scholarship," Elli interjected.

"That's right. They gave scholarships to less qualified students," I scoffed.

"Why was that?"

"It's because he was baturé—half black and half white," Elli replied. "Maybe they felt that Ibrahim could count on the money of an absent white father."

"Did Ibrahim find out about you?" Mamadou asked me.

"He knew that his white father lived in the United States and sent money for his education. That's all. He never saw a photo of me and didn't know what I did for a living. And that," I said, sighing, "was very hard to take."

"Tell them about the others," Elli suggested.

"You remember Mariama and Adam?"

"Of course," said Mamadou.

"They did well. Mariama sent me letters and photos all the time. A year or two after I left Niger, she expanded the Fofo Bar into a restaurant. Several years later she moved the Fofo Bar/Restaurant to the center of Niamey. Adam attended the same private middle school and high school as Ibrahim."

"Did they know one another?"

"It's hard to say," I said. "They probably did. There are not too many baturé at those schools." I paused a moment to wonder once more how well Ibrahim and Adam knew one another. Might they have been in the same classes? Did they eat lunch together or go to the cinema in the same group? "But I have no way of knowing."

"And what became of Adam?" Mamadou asked.

The thought of Adam made me swell with pride. "He grew tall and strong and became a good student. But his real passion was soccer. He played center forward for the high school team, and every season he scored many goals. He enrolled at the university in Niamey and plays for Niamey's most famous soccer club."

"True?" Mamadou exclaimed.

"Absolutely."

"Did he remember you?"

"He remembers that I gave him his first soccer ball. We've been close ever since."

"And what about Elli?" Mamadou asked. "You've hardly spoken about her."

The ring of the telephone interrupted the conversation. Elli picked up the phone and retreated to the back room.

"For that we must return to Niger. Many years have passed . . ."

NIGER 1991

The stuffiness of the room made me want to yawn, but I resisted the inclination. Seated in front of perhaps seventy-five people at the American Cultural Center in Niamey, Niger, I did not want to suggest that I was bored. Although I disliked public speaking, I had been invited as a Fulbright lecturer, and of course I had to present lectures. The three-week summer lectureship, however, gave me time to see my friends in Niger. I had already spent considerable time arranging shipments with Diop, my longtime business partner. A four-day trip to Tillaberi had brought me great pleasure.

That night I was going to talk about the geometric designs found in West African textiles. I had brought many colorful slides of cloth and looms as well as photo portraits of Amadu and Seyni. Regrettably, Amadu, my teacher, had died in 1988. Since then Seyni had proudly taken on his father's burden. My books had brought Amadu and Seyni modest royalties as well as some degree of recognition. Seyni and I were like brothers.

The embassy's cultural attaché, James Smith III, a short, skinny man in a shapeless gray suit, stood at the podium. He wore thick glasses and spoke at length about my work. "Professor Lyons," he was saying, with a somewhat stilted accent, "was among the first scholars to decode the complex symbolism of West African textile patterns." I had a hard time listening to lengthy introductions. To me, the mock seriousness of a ritualized testimonial sounded more like an obituary than an introduction. My mind drifted back to the past.

I mused about my life in America. I had built a good life for myself. I loved my twelfth-floor apartment, which overlooked Riverside

Park in New York City. From this high vantage, I could happily watch the first rays of light illumine the sweep of the Hudson River. Typically, I read the *New York Times* over coffee and had a bagel with Nova Scotia Lox from Murray's, the best fish shop in all of New York. If it was a teaching day, I set off on the long journey to Bendix College, a liberal arts institution in Somerset County, New Jersey. The college, which in the past fifteen years had attracted a highly diverse student population, was named after the Bendix Corporation, the manufacturers of those indestructible washing machines of yore. Some of my colleagues liked to say that the actor William Bendix had been the college's major benefactor. In the old days the college did have what may be called a *Life of Riley* atmosphere. For the past twenty years, however, the administration had offered a curriculum that appealed to diversity. They had hired me, after all, to teach art history and African studies. Several of my colleagues referred to the school as "the Harvard of Somerset County." During my dozen years there, my courses had attracted large numbers of students.

My commute, like much of my life, was tediously regular. During the academic year, I traveled to campus three times a week, taking the subway to Penn Station, the train to Bernardsville, and then a shuttle to Bendix. After more than an hour in trains and buses, I'd arrive at the main campus gate, a tall black iron, doweled structure consisting of one six-foot-wide door that closed on a gate jamb decorated at the top with swirling gold leaf. A kiosk next to the gate displayed in bold letters the college's name. Beneath the name, a message board announced the day's events: "Phi Kappa Sigma meeting, 3:30 p.m., 101 Stetson Hall"; "Freshman Orientation Assembly, 10:00 a.m., 100 Applegate Hall." The gate was squeezed between imposing eight-foot stone walls that enclosed the entire campus and, combined with the college's gothic-style buildings, also built of stone, gave Bendix the look of a medieval town.

A sweep of stone buildings formed an ellipse around a quadrangle that had a mass of beautifully manicured lawns and sidewalks bordered by shrubbery and flowering trees. At the end farthest from the gate stood the imposing library, which was flanked on one side by the towered and turreted Administration Building and on the other by the drab and dark square angles of the Humanities Building, the site of my office.

I always arrived thirty minutes before my Introduction to African Studies course was scheduled to meet. I would enter the Humanities Building and walk up the creaky stairs to the third floor. The ceilings were high and fissured, the corridors wide and dimly lit. Students had plastered the walls with posters about upcoming lectures, advertisements for courses, lecture announcements, conference placards, items for sale, and rooms to share.

I would then come upon the Humanities Division's central office, the station of Mrs. Holt, the departmental secretary. She was a tall, imposing woman of sixty years with blue-white hair teased up for increased body. Despite her air of propriety, she loved to tease people, especially me. For years we had enjoyed a repartee akin to the West African joking relationship, in which the partners tease and insult one another but never take offense. Despite the joking, I respected Mrs. Holt's considerable abilities. She sensed this squarely and provided me with more than a fair share of her time.

I would then check my mailbox and saunter down to my office, my sanctuary at Bendix. The office was the size of a large living room in a pricey suburban house. Four large casement windows offered a view of the quadrangle. On sunny days the office was awash in light, which made my plants—a ficus tree, assorted ferns, and a rubber plant—smile with growth. One of my office walls was lined with built-in bookshelves that contained my books as well as strategically placed pieces of African art that Diop had found for me over the years. Another wall was adorned with West African textiles: a large piece of antique kente cloth—blue, red, green, and gold dyed silk woven in intricate stripe patterns—and a Fulan blanket, red, black, green, and gold threads woven into geometric squares. Between the textiles I displayed my photographs—portraits of Amadu and Seyni at work on their looms, Nigerien landscapes, and Diop seated in front of his art stall. Two oriental carpets covered the hardwood floor—a red and blue pile rug from Iran and a Turkish kilim that featured dark red, light blue, and black strips overlaid with white squares and triangles. Life in Niger had taught me to savor the wonder of light. When I burned Meccan incense in the office, I'd sometimes close my eyes and imagine myself in the Tillaberi or Niamey market. My life had been sweet, I mused, drifting back to the irritating drone of James Smith III's creaky voice, except for the fact that I had no one with whom to share it.

"I now have the great pleasure," Smith continued, "to present Dr. David Lyons."

The crowd applauded with courteous restraint. I stood and approached the podium. I peppered my standard talk about textile designs with funny stories about Amadu and Seyni in Tillaberi and showed slides—quite striking if I do say so myself—of textiles and looms. The audience laughed at my attempts at humorous storytelling and gave me a warm round of applause at the lecture's end. Several people asked me questions about weaving designs and weaving technique.

James Smith III limply shook my hand. "Dr. Lyons, I must say that your talk was most informative."

I itched to escape to the bonhomie of Diop's house. "Thanks," I said half-heartedly. I then noticed a tall woman with long black hair walking toward us. She wore a black skirt, a black top, and a simple but striking silver necklace.

"Are you going to introduce me, James?"

Flustered by the woman's presence, Smith awkwardly made introductions.

"Dr. Lyons . . ."

"James," I said, "this is Africa. Call me David."

"Okay. David, I'd like to introduce you to Elli Farouch."

Immediately attracted to this woman, I shook her hand. "It's a pleasure to meet you."

She smiled. "I thoroughly enjoyed the lecture. What a pleasure it must be to work with people like Amadu and Seyni."

"I'm grateful to know such people," I agreed.

"Uh, Elli here," James inserted, "is our post psychologist." He snickered. "She keeps us on the up and up."

I smiled. "Is that so?"

"You bet," Elli said.

James departed to work the rest of the room, leaving Elli and me alone.

"Would you be free for drinks?" I asked.

"When?"

"Are you free now?"

"I am. Let's go to the bar at the Grand Hotel. It's quiet there."

THIRTY-SEVEN

We found a table in the corner of the Grand Hotel's bar, a sleek room filled with low wooden tables and soft high-backed chairs covered in black velvet. "I'm a wine drinker," I announced.

"So am I."

"Do you want white wine?"

"That's what I drink."

I waved to the waiter. "Do you have white wines from Burgundy?"

"You're in luck, Monsieur. We have some excellent Macon-Viré."

I ordered a bottle and looked across the table at the elegant Elli. "You've heard my spiel. What's yours?"

She laughed. "I have no spiel, but I'll tell you something of myself. I was born in Lebanon. My people are Muslim cloth merchants, and I grew up speaking Arabic and French. When the war came to Lebanon, we moved to Paris, where my parents opened a cloth shop. My aunts, uncles, and cousins helped us, and we did well. As for me, I was a good student in high school—English was my favorite subject. Then I went to the Sorbonne and studied psychology."

"So," I interjected, as the waiter brought the wine, "you learned your psychology in France?"

Elli took a sip of her wine. "That's very good wine." She smiled at me. "I learned some of my psychology in France. You see, I didn't want to stay in France, so I went to New York to study at the New School. New York is a tough place to be a student—so expensive. So it took me a while to get my degree. To pay my tuition and get by, I worked nights at a psychiatric hospital." She twisted her hair. "You know how it is." She paused to sip more wine. "My parents always taught me to be persistent but patient. That's how I got my degree and went into practice."

By this time, I had already downed two glasses of wine. I topped off Elli's glass and emptied the rest of the bottle into my own goblet. "You practiced in New York?"

"I did for a while. Then I met my husband, Phillip Walden Walker II, a diplomat in the State Department."

I blinked. "You're married?"

"For now, I'm separated."

"Do all State Department people have names like James Smith III and Philip Walden Walker II?" I asked. "It sounds so aristocratic."

Elli laughed. "Not all of them."

"What happened?"

"You mean to my marriage?"

"Yes."

"I fell in love with his easy-going manner. He was the opposite of the people in my family—crazy Lebanese."

"What happened then?"

"We got along fine. We lived in Turkey, India, and Morocco. He scored career points as a political officer and I worked as a post psychologist."

By now a second bottle of Macon-Viré had arrived. The waiter poured me another glass. Elli's previous glass hadn't been touched. "It sounds like a sweet life."

Elli nodded. "It was a good life, but my husband lacked passion. I wanted someone who was full of life, not someone who wanted to be left alone."

"So?"

"So he got posted to Washington and I asked for the psychologist position here. They sent me here eleven months ago."

By now my head felt warm and a bit numb. I poured myself another glass of wine. It was my turn to talk. I started to tell stories about my youthful days in Africa. I told her about how Stevie Hunter, who had become a vice president at Chase Manhattan Bank, had started me on the path of youthful delights. I described how Bobby Claggett, now a trouble-shooting consultant in disaster relief, dragged me through bank after bank of marijuana fog on our hike from Tillaberi to Ouallam.

"Sounds like you were pretty wild."

"I wasn't as wild as my friends."

"I'm going to order some Arak," Elli said. "Do you know it?"

"It's from Lebanon?"

"You want to try some?"

I downed my glass of Arak in one gulp and lost all restraint. I told her about Amadu and Seyni, Zeinabou and Ibrahim, the interminable tension between desire and obligation, and my inability to make a commitment to my girlfriends in New Haven. I recounted the sad story of my return to Niger, my search for Zeinabou and Ibrahim, my discovery of Mariama and Adam, and how serendipity intervened to bring me face-to-face with my former girlfriend. I described the sorrow I felt upon seeing a photo of Ibrahim and realizing that the young boy was, indeed, my son. Then I lapsed into incoherence.

Taking pity on a large and inebriated man, Elli took my limp body to her apartment, laid me down on the living room sofa, and covered me with a blanket.

THIRTY-EIGHT

I woke to the sounds of wind-rattled windows in Elli's apartment. Heavy rain splattering on the roof sounded like a stampede. My head throbbed, my nose ached, and my eyes seemed small in their sockets, as the French would say. Slowly I opened my eyes and saw Elli looking at me. She was so beautiful in her black tank top and short skirt.

My face suddenly felt hot. "I'm so sorry. I made a mess of everything. I can't believe I got so drunk."

"You were pretty far gone, but very funny. You told so many stories."

"I don't remember any of them."

"They were great."

I sat up. "I never get drunk. You know, I can drink a whole bottle of wine and not even feel high." I scratched my head and rubbed my eyes.

"It must have been the Arak. My ancestors made strong stuff."

"I'll say. I haven't been that drunk in years."

"Would you like some strong coffee?"

"That would be great."

"I'll bring some coffee." She walked toward the kitchen.

"Elli?"

She turned around.

"You look beautiful this morning." I couldn't believe what I had just said. I was usually much more restrained—especially with women.

"Thank you, David," she said, smiling warmly. "I'll get the coffee."

For some unfathomable reason, I felt completely at home in Elli's apartment. From the moment I met her, I inexplicably wanted to share my deepest secrets with her. And although I had long overstayed my welcome, I didn't want to leave.

Elli brought a tray with coffee, bread, feta cheese, olives, tomatoes, and sliced cucumber. "Drink your coffee. This food will settle your stomach."

"I'm so sorry to put you to all this trouble," I said.

"What trouble?" she replied. "I'll back in a minute. I need to brew some tea."

When she came back, I slowly got off the sofa and walked unsteadily to the table. "My God, I'm a mess. Please forgive me."

"Drink your coffee. Eat some vegetables. And then drink lots of tea. Tea will fix you up."

"That sounds like good advice."

After breakfast I didn't know what to do. I still wanted to stay with Elli, but felt awkward. "I guess I need to go home."

"I can take you, if you like," she said.

When I got to my furnished efficiency apartment, I felt like an alien. It had cheap furniture and bare white walls. "I hate it here," I admitted.

"How much longer will you stay in Niger?" Elli asked.

"I've got two more weeks."

"Gather your things and bring them to my house. You can stay there—on the couch."

I wanted to accept this kind invitation, but felt it would be bad form to do so. "Thanks so much, but I can't impose on you like that."

"It's not an imposition."

We returned to Elli's with my things. The apartment looked out over a garden. She had a black leather sofa and had covered the parquet floor with several Turkish and Afghan kilims. On one wall of the salon there was a small collection of masks from Côte d'Ivoire. On the other wall Elli had hung a Songhay textile. "I see you have masks and blankets."

"Yes," Elli said from the kitchen. "I'm passionate about African art. I like being a psychologist, but I don't want to spend my whole life listening to clients. That's why I came to your lecture. While you're here, I'm going to pump you for information."

"You know," I said, "I'm also an African art trader. My partner, Diop, lives here in Niamey. If you like, I'll introduce you to him."

"That would be terrific."

I heard the sizzle of meat in cooking oil. "May I come into the kitchen?"

"Of course you can." Elli turned over a flat kabob. A cucumber, tomato, and onion salad had already been mixed in a bowl, and a pot of rice steamed on the stove. Spices made the kitchen smell like a bazaar. "This food will chase away your hangover."

I drank four glasses of water and helped myself to three portions of food. Slowly, my hangover began to retreat. While I cleared the table and washed the dishes, Elli played her favorite Miles Davis CD, *Kind of Blue*. I was putting the last glass away, when Elli came up behind me, put her hands on my shoulders, and turned me around. She kissed me and began to unbutton my shirt. "You don't mind if I do this, do you?"

She led me to the bedroom. We spent the afternoon making love, my hangover now a fading memory.

THIRTY-NINE

The next evening I took Elli to Diop's house. She had been seeing clients at the embassy all day. I had used the morning to prepare a lecture that I would soon give at the Université de Niamey. In the afternoon, I took a break and went to see friends at the Grand Marché. Elli had not spent much time in Diop's part of Niamey, which was more crowded than her "European" neighborhood. I parked Elli's car under a tree just to the right of Diop's door. Smoke from cooking fires rose to form a thick cloud above the sandy street. Children frolicked in the street. Nose-wrinkling smells of rotting food mixed with the savory aroma of roasting meat.

I clapped three times at Diop's door.

"Praise to God!" a female voice called out. "David is here! David is here! Come in, brother-in-law."

We entered to find Fatou Diop, round, fleshy, and beautiful in a deep blue caftan. Ignoring my familiar face, she went right up to Elli. "Welcome to my house, David's friend. Tonight you will eat well and laugh a great deal."

"And me? What about my greeting?" I asked.

She waved her hand at me and continued to look at Elli. "These men are never satisfied, my sister. Never!"

"You're right about that, Madame Diop," Elli said.

"Please, call me Fatou."

Diop walked into the courtyard, which appeared to be in its normal state of disarray: pots and pans lying here and there; chickens wandering about; children, some belonging to Diop, running after one another; statuettes leaning against window frames and door jambs as if keeping a vigil. Even though several years had passed since my last visit, Diop looked the same—only a little bit bigger, a little bit thicker. His bulky presence still commanded any space that he occupied, and yet his bulk still suggested sweetness instead of swagger.

"Welcome to my house, Elli. Any friend of David is my friend." He showed Elli and me to a table that had been put under one of the compound's acacias. Four places had been set. "Tonight we eat *thiebudan*. Two days ago, my wife received some special spices from Dakar. She has been cooking the stew for hours."

"I've had *thieb* in a restaurant," Elli said.

"Ah," said Diop, "and did you like it?"

"Delicious."

"Tonight you'll taste homemade *thieb* and tell me what you think."

Fatou joined us at the table, and soon thereafter helpers brought the food: a substantial mound of rice cooked in tomato sauce on a large platter, with chunks of fish, cabbage, carrots, and turnips; whole peppers; and pieces of eggplant arranged on top of the mound. We ate and ate and ate. After a while, Fatou Diop excused herself and disappeared into the kitchen.

When we had eaten an acceptably large portion of the food,

helpers took it away. Diop then passed around a bowl of water, and we all took deep drinks.

"Praise be to God," I proclaimed.

"The food was wonderful," Elli interjected.

"Thanks. But you have to tell my wife when she comes back. "

Elli stood up. "I'll tell her right now."

Diop leaned over to me. "I like this woman very much. She has spirit, but she is also kind-hearted."

"She's fantastic," I said, "but I haven't known her very long."

"Keep her in your life, my friend. She'll be good for you. I can sense these things."

Diop did, in fact, have uncanny instincts about a person's character. This ability helped him immeasurably in his business. "Can we show Elli the wood?"

"Of course," Diop said, looking toward the kitchen. "Ah, here she comes now."

We went into the storeroom. Diop turned on a light that dimly illuminated an area stuffed with African art. Masks covered every inch of wall space. Some of the carvings had the form of human faces, others represented animals, and still other depicted spirits. Elli blindly walked farther into the room and knocked over a statue.

"Oh, I'm so sorry."

"Not to worry," said Diop nonchalantly, "it happens all the time. The one you knocked over is a Baulé grandfather from Côte d'Ivoire." Diop chuckled. "He hasn't had that much attention from a woman in a very long time."

Quietly overwhelmed, Elli stood in the middle of the room. "How can you live with so many eyes looking at you? It makes me wonder about their past. Who carved them? Who owned them? Did people dance to them or make offerings to them? Right now, I feel like hundreds of people are looking at me."

"David used to sleep in this room," Diop said.

Elli turned to me. "You're kidding! How could anyone sleep in this room?"

I shrugged. "You get used to it. You may not believe this, but African statues and masks have always given me comfort. When I stayed here, I slept very soundly."

Elli looked at Diop. "You know, these pieces could bring you a great deal of money in America. Reproductions sell well, and originals even better."

"You've got good instincts," Diop told her.

"My people are Lebanese merchants."

"Very good instincts," Diop said.

We exited the storeroom and saw Fatou Diop standing by a low table arrayed with small tea glasses and a bowl of sugar. "Come and drink tea," she commanded.

We sat down on leather pillows that had been placed on a palm-frond mat under a fragrant eucalyptus tree. Diop put a measure of green tea in the pot and put the pot on a brazier filled with glowing charcoals. "We'll drink tea and talk."

He turned to Elli. "I like your Lebanese instincts." He gestured toward me. "My friend here knows art very well—especially cloth—but he has no head for business."

"It's true," I admitted. "We find wonderful pieces, Diop ships them to me, and we have trouble selling them for good prices."

"Why is that?" Elli asked.

Diop had an answer. "It's simple. David isn't good at selling. We need someone in America who can sell." He paused to mix the tea and sugar and then served us. A moment later he picked up his glass of tea. "We need someone like you, Elli. You could learn about the art." He smiled. "I don't think anyone has to teach you how to sell."

"But Elli is a psychologist," I interjected. "And she works here, not in America."

"Not for much longer." She sipped her tea. "I've always wanted to do something like this."

Diop raised his hands above his head. "You see, David. You see."

"I return to America in four weeks," Elli continued. "I'm going to work as a psychologist in New York, but that will leave me time to work with you."

Up to this point, my life had been like a rumpled blanket: comfortable but in disarray. In a mere two days, Elli had smoothed the blanket, making it both comfortable and complete. "What do you have in mind?" I asked.

"We could open an African art gallery," said Elli in a confident voice.

"A wonderful idea," said Diop.

"I have friends and family who can help with financing. I'll find a space and arrange it. And you two," she said, gesturing to Diop and me, "will deal with supply and shipment."

I felt like pinching myself to make sure that this moment was, indeed, real. Was my life really beginning to change? Elli would continue to treat clients in New York. I would continue to teach. In our spare time, we would live our passion. I had many doubts, of course. Would these wonderful possibilities result in yet another series of disappointments? Would there ever be an art gallery in New York? Having known Elli for only two days, but feeling a sense of comfort and confidence that usually developed from a lifelong relationship, I felt with uncanny certainty that our lives would be happily linked for many years to come. For some reason, I also knew that we'd soon open a gallery. "What should we call the gallery?" I asked.

Diop didn't hesitate. "We'll call it Gallery Bundu. I'll be there for the opening."

FORTY

Two days later in the late afternoon, I took Elli to see the Fofo Bar/ Restaurant, now located on the ground floor of a three-story office building and only a short walk from Diop's art stall. We found Mariama sitting on one of the tall black barstools. The bar, long, black, and gleaming and shaped like the letter L, ran parallel to one wall. Beyond the bar there was a door, probably to the kitchen. A polished parquet dance floor, square and at the very center of the space, separated the bar from about twenty tables, all covered with damask tablecloths. Each table had four place settings—bone china, white linen napkins, silverware, and glasses for water and wine. A small bandstand hugged the establishment's back wall.

Mariama looked up from her books, smiled at us, and nodded. "Now I understand why you haven't been here for a while."

"Mariama," I said. "This is Elli Farouch, my friend."

Mariama and Elli shook hands.

"Since I've been here," I said to Elli, "I've eaten here just about every night."

"David and I are like brother and sister," Mariama stated. "If you are David's friend, you are my sister. Come here anytime and eat. You can try to pay, but I will not take your money."

Elli smiled. "You talk like my Lebanese relatives."

Mariama glanced sideways at me and gave me a wink. She then looked at Elli. "You know, Elli, David is part of my family. My son and I have had difficult times, but David always looked after us—even when he's been far away. As soon as I met him, I knew we'd be close for the rest of our lives. And that's the way it's been." She spread out her arms. "David is a good man."

"Thanks, Mariama, but you're the one who made the restaurant work." I turned to Elli. "And she's hired a great cook who prepares wonderful food."

Just then Adam bounded into the Fofo. He was big and bronze with thick curly black hair. Jeans and a white T-shirt labeled "Reebok" hugged his muscular body. He ambled up to us and hit me on the arm. "Well, Uncle," he said, "when am I going to get you onto the soccer field?" He playfully grabbed my head, put it in a vice lock, and released me. "So when will it be, coach?"

"I'm too old for that," I protested.

He waved his hand. "I know men even older than you who play."

"Maybe we can take a bike ride on the road to Say?"

Adam pointed his forefinger at me. "You're on. We'll go tomorrow?"

"Tomorrow," I said.

Adam turned toward Elli. "You are much too young and beautiful to be friends with an old man like Uncle David."

Elli smiled demurely and winked at Adam. "He seems pretty energetic to me."

Adam put his arm around me and said to Elli. "You know, it is hard to be a baturé in Niger. People say terrible things. Sometimes they make you feel like an animal." He tightened his grip around me. "Uncle David helped me. He gave me my first soccer ball. He read to me. He wrote me two letters a month for many, many years and sent me to a private school. Now I study at the university and play soccer for a club here in Niamey. Maybe next month I'll be named, inshallah, to Niger's national team."

"May God accept that," I said in Songhay.

Mariama stepped off the barstool. The years had been kind to her. Her skin remained smooth and clear, and her tall, slender frame looked elegant in a tight-fitting white sleeveless top and long black skirt. "Elli," she said, "you and David must join Adam and me for dinner. Sit down and have a glass of wine. We'll eat later."

FORTY-ONE

After a sumptuous meal of chicken groundnut stew over rice and several glasses of white wine, Elli and I drove back to the apartment. Elli put on some jazz. "Sit down, David. I'm going to make some herbal tea."

The melodious piano of "Monk's Dream" soon filled the room. I closed my eyes and let the music take me away. I thought immediately of Amadu, who had died three years earlier, and heard his soft, raspy voice going on about warp and weft, desire and obligation, and how weavers patiently recreated the world through their works. Just then I realized the depth of Amadu's wisdom and counted myself lucky to have known such a man. Like Amadu, I had tried to meet my obligations. I too had been patient. I too had tried, in my own way, to weave the world. A sinuous path lay before me. Smiling inwardly, I saw that I would continue to combine warp and weft to recreate the world. Warmth spread through my limbs.

Elli brought in a brass platter with tea glasses, a steaming teapot, and a bowl of sugar cubes. She sat down next to me and poured tea into glasses.

"Drink," she said. "This is mint tea, the medicine of my ancestors."

I smiled at her and sipped my tea.

"You seem so close to Mariama and Adam," Elli observed.

"I've known them a long time. It was strange, but even the first time I met them, I felt like I was with family."

"When that happens," Elli said, "it's wonderful."

"It's been great," I said, sipping more tea, "to watch Adam grow up."

"What about Ibrahim?"

Elli's question hit me like a blow to the head. I had had such a fine evening. Why was she asking me about Ibrahim? "What about him?"

"Don't you ever wonder what your son is like?"

This question made my stomach quiver. How many times had I wondered about Ibrahim? What might he be like? Who were his friends? What were his passions? Sadly, I had no clue. "Sometimes I do," I answered. "I've got no idea what he's like. I saw his picture many years ago, but I don't even know what he looks like now or what kind of person he's become."

"Don't you want to find out?" Elli asked.

Elli's persistence angered me. What did she know about my pain and sense of loss? But I also realized that Elli's tenaciousness had not been pernicious but a reflection of her concern about my well-being. Even though we had not known each other very long, I knew then that Elli loved me. This revelation eased the tension in my arms and legs and cleared the confusion in my mind. "Yes, I want to find out about him, but I'm afraid of what I'll discover."

"You fear rejection," she stated.

"Damn right I do."

"But can you go through the rest of your life not knowing about your son?"

"No I can't."

"If that's so, what do you plan to do about it?"

I loved and admired Elli's determined way of facing problems. You identify the problem, confront it, and then you do your best to resolve it, one way or another.

FORTY-TWO

The next day Elli lent me her Renault. I dropped her off at the embassy in the morning and then drove directly to the central market to see if Zeinabou still owned the cloth boutique. As I drove past the Presidential Palace, I thought about how and why so much had changed in Niger. There were so many people and so much traffic in Niamey. A sprawling, chaotic city had grown out of what had been a contained, peaceful town. People from the bush who were poor and hungry had come to the city seeking a better life, only to find squalor and destitution. When I finally came upon the central market, I envisioned its former sinuous pathways and makeshift wooden stalls. Several years earlier the old market had mysteriously burned to the ground. On the same site, the government had built a market with straight pathways and concrete structures. The new market featured numbered stalls, a water system to keep the passageways free of trash and garbage, and even a police tower that reminded me of a spherical spaceship on a spindle-like landing pod. So much had changed in Niger. After my absence of all these years, would Zeinabou still be in business?

I drove into a dusty parking space opposite the market. To my right I noticed a Lebanese grocery store. To my left rose the sand-stained white facade of the American Cultural Center, the site of my lecture several days earlier. Before me I saw the cloth shop. In the window mannequins had been outfitted in the latest fashions—both African and European. A sign above the door read "Bonkono Cloth Shop." For several minutes I sat in the car and stared at the boutique. Even though I had been in this neighborhood several times on this visit, I had avoided the cloth shop—out of fear. Better not to know about bad news, I told myself. Well, the cloth shop was still there, and maybe Zeinabou was still the owner.

As soon as I opened the car door, a young man with wasted legs moved my way on a hand-pedaled tricycle that had been fashioned from scrap. He wore a torn white T-shirt, a pair of oversized khaki shorts, and a big smile. "Monsieur, you need a guardian for your car. There are many thieves here. I'll protect your car." The boy held out his hand. "We got a deal?"

I shook the boy's hand. "We've got a deal," I said in Songhay. Some things never change.

The boy beamed. "I give a special rate for the white man who speaks Songhay."

"No special rate for me, my friend."

The boy nodded. "No one touches your car."

I walked into the boutique. Zeinabou, large and shapeless under her black caftan, stood behind the counter. On seeing me, she arched her back and stared at me. Feeling an almost youthful boldness, I began our conversation. "It's been a long time, Zeinabou—many years." I took a few steps forward. "I see you're still in business."

"Praise be to God," she said.

"You're a remarkable woman."

"It's through the grace of Allah that I have made my way."

"You've become religious?"

"Yes. My ancestors were pious Muslims, and now I follow their way. After years of wandering, I've finally come to my senses."

I wondered if this conversion meant that she'd be more forthcoming. I smiled. "I'm beginning to come to mine."

"That's good," she said. Zeinabou shrugged what had become rather large shoulders. "What brings you here?"

In the past Zeinabou's no-nonsense directness had intimidated me. Feeling more self-assured, I now found it less disturbing. I stood erect and looked directly into Zeinabou's eyes. "I want to see my son."

"After so many years, you're still interested in Ibrahim?" she asked sarcastically.

I moved closer to the mother of my son. "He's my son."

Zeinabou pursed her lips. "Can you be so sure?"

The depth of Zeinabou's anger seemed bottomless, but was it anger or perhaps a lack of respect? No matter the emotional source of her resentment, a response in kind would only reinforce her lack of respect for me. I decided to remain calm, but forceful. "Yes, I can," I said evenly. "There's no doubt." I paused a moment. "When can I see him?"

The cool response sent a barely visible shudder through Zeinabou's body. She sat down on a stool behind the counter, and her shoulders slumped. "I don't want you to see him, but," she said taking a deep breath, "I'm a Muslim woman now and it is not our way to keep a father from his son."

Ever skeptical, I wondered just how much Islam had changed her. I moved a step closer. "He's in town?"

"Yes," she said, looking at the countertop. "He's been in France all year—in Paris at the university, but he's come back here for the summer. They put him to work at the Foreign Affairs Ministry." She looked up at me. "Ibrahim has made me proud. He's always been the best student in his classes. He was the best student at the lycée, but they didn't give him a university scholarship." She paused. "They refused him because he's a baturé."

"That's horrible," I said. "But he's managed to go to Paris, anyway?"

"Business has been good, thank God." She coughed. "And your money has helped."

"Does Ibrahim know about me?"

"Once he got older, I told him a little. Just before he left for Paris, he said that if you ever came back to Niamey, he'd like to meet you."

"After all these years, why does he want to meet me now?"

"Put yourself in his place." A customer walking in caught Zeinabou's attention. "If you want to meet him, go to the Grand Hotel veranda tomorrow evening at six o'clock. You'll recognize one another."

"Thank you," I said.

Exhausted, I left the boutique. The car had been well guarded, the young man having positioned his tricycle next to the driver's door. He chewed on a stick.

The prospect of meeting my son both elated and frightened me. What would I say to Ibrahim? How might I explain myself? How would he respond to me? What could I expect from such a meeting? I decided that I'd try to be as cool and self-assured as I could in such circumstances. It had worked well with Zeinabou. It might work well with Ibrahim. "I see you've done good work," I told the boy in Songhay.

"Only the best service for you, Monsieur."

"Only the best payment for you," I countered. I gave the boy three thousand francs—an astronomical sum for guardian services.

FORTY-THREE

I arrived at the Grand Hotel terrace well before my six o'clock meeting with Ibrahim. I sat down at a shady table overlooking the Niger

River basin. The overnight rain made the river look like an angry brown snake. The river's rusty brown contrasted sharply with the dark green of freshly nourished bush grasses and plants. The clear and bright late-afternoon light illuminated even the smallest details of the landscape that stretched out beneath me. A copper-hued mountain curled up from the green plain. Rock shelters cast long shadows along one of the mountain's ridges. The motion of the world slowed down. A formation of ducks free-floated over the river, and a dove call echoed in the distance. I could hear the murmur of conversation, but at a slow speed—like an old forty-five rpm record played at thirty-three speed. A waiter in a starched white uniform, black and gold epaulets, and a red sash, moved toward me in what seemed slow but giant strides.

"Monsieur," he said politely. "What will you have?"

"I'd like a Ricard."

"That's a good choice."

On hot afternoons I always loved to listen to the blues and drink Ricard, the anise cocktail from Marseilles. It was my friend Dédé Bergerac who had first introduced me to the pleasures of Ricard. Normally Dédé mixed one part Ricard to four parts water, which produced a white milky liquid that smelled like licorice. When I once suffered from a severe case of dysentery, Dédé mixed me a straight Ricard. In my mind's eye, I saw Dédé holding up that cocktail glass to examine it.

"You know, the Fulan think milk is their medicine," Dédé had said. "In the south of France, Ricard is our medicine. Drink it and it will kill what ails your gut."

Sitting in the splendor of that terrace, I wondered what had become of Dédé. I had heard that my French friend had fallen passionately in love with a Mexican woman who wanted to share a life with him in sunny Mexico. But Dédé had elected to remain in France—in rainy and damp Rouen, where he taught primary school. Although he missed his beloved Toulouse, he eventually married a woman from Rouen and remained there. In short order he became a father to a daughter and a son. Dédé played rugby for Rouen for several years and then coached the Rouen team. By now his children would be teenagers. I wondered if he was still married. Did he still hate the climate, cuisine, and culture of Normandy? Had social obligation required a life that he didn't want? Why do we make choices, I wondered, that make us miserable?

The waiter brought me my drink. I held the glass in the air and looked at the milky liquid. Dédé's straight Ricard hadn't worked, all those years ago; it burned like hell on the way down and settled in the pit of my stomach, where it provoked sharp cramps and violent diarrhea. "It's your weak American intestines," Dédé had said. "Your country's too damn sanitary."

Filled with these memories, I sipped the Ricard. The afternoon light had become deeper, almost golden. A western breeze cooled the air. Below me a solitary fisherman glided his dugout downstream. I thought of the choices I had made. What would have happened had I remained in Niger with Zeinabou? I could have easily found work and lived with her and Ibrahim. But would I have been happy? She was a strong, stubborn, and independent woman whose view of the world was quite different from my own. We would have doubtless had a stormy relationship. Besides, I would have held her responsible for curtailing my education and stifling my professional ambitions. Perhaps leaving had been the right thing to do? I shook my head at these thoughts and ordered a second Ricard. The real issue for me was not Zeinabou, but Ibrahim. Of all people, I knew what it was like to grow up without a father, and I felt guilty that my youthful choices had sealed the same fate for my own son. What a cruel irony! Like my friend Dédé, I had been torn between obligation and desire. There was a difference, though. Unlike my French friend, I had torn the blanket of social obligation. My financial contributions to Zeinabou, Ibrahim, Mariama, and Adam had been an attempt to mend the tear in the blanket. And yet I knew from Amadu's teachings that the mended blanket lacks force; it is easily torn again. How much mending can one do? What would Amadu say about my years of mending? Amadu would speak to me simply and directly. He'd tell me that it was time to take possession of my loom and weave a new blanket.

"Professor Lyons? Professor Lyons?"

I turned and saw a tall, thin young man with thick curly black hair. He had my eyes, nose, and mouth—a dark copy of me as a young man. My heart thumped in my chest and sweat beaded on my brow. What should I say to my . . . ?

"Professor Lyons?"

"Yes?"

"May I sit down?"

"Please, sit down."

We stared at one another in mutual recognition. Who would speak first? What would be said?

"Do you want something to drink?" I asked.

"I'll have a Bière Niger."

I ordered a beer for Ibrahim.

"My mother said you'd be here."

The waiter poured beer into a glass. Ibrahim took a sip and looked into my eyes, a slight smile on his face.

I leaned toward Ibrahim. "Could you call me something other than Professor Lyons?"

Ibrahim took another sip and sat rigidly in his chair. "What should I call you? Should I call you father? Just what should I call you?"

"Call me David," I said, trying to remain calm.

"How can I call you David? We don't know one another."

"Look, I don't expect . . ."

Ibrahim's body shuddered as if jolted by electricity. His voice then took on the calm tone of deep-seated anger. "Expect . . . You have no idea what it's like to grow up as a bastard baturé in Niger. You never fit in. The kids call you a half-breed, and the adults keep you away from their children. The only thing you get to know is loneliness. In school, they don't honor you even though you're the best student in the class. You realize that you are different and that fills you with sadness and rage. The rage burns in your gut because you have no father to love and protect you. You have no father to show you the way." He paused a moment. "Can you understand that?"

"I can't."

Ibrahim slumped back in his chair and finished his glass of beer. "So you see," he said in an almost breathless tone, "it's difficult to know what to call you." He poured more beer into his glass. "The only way to survive my kind of life is to escape."

"Do you like France?"

"That's right. In France I'm free."

"What are you studying there?" I asked, trying to steer the conversation to more neutral topics.

"Political economy," Ibrahim said. "I like Marx and Fanon. I also demonstrate in the streets, mostly against American neocolonialism."

"Do you have an idea what you want to be?"

"I'd like to be a good father," he said dispassionately.

"That," I said, sighing, "is what's important, isn't it?"

My attempt at humility softened Ibrahim a bit. "Yes it is."

"Do you want another beer?"

"I could use another."

I ordered another beer for Ibrahim. I had harbored no illusions about the meeting. I knew that we would never experience the joys and strains of a father-son relationship. Even so, I was relieved to have met my son, if only for a brief moment.

"Do you know why I called you Professor Lyons?" Ibrahim asked.

"I have no idea. . . . Why?"

"It's because I've read your work. When my mother told me about you and your research, I wanted to know more about the man who left us. So I read your work on weaving."

"You've read my work?" I asked with great surprise.

"Yes. If only you could have respected my mother and me the way you respected your weavers!"

"I've made many mistakes."

"Yes, you have, David."

Hearing my name from my son's lips sounded sweet to me, but I allowed myself no illusions about Ibrahim. "I believe that someday you'll make a good father, Ibrahim."

"I'll try my best. I also want to be a professor."

Ibrahim stood up, took a long look at me, and turned to leave.

"Ibrahim?" I called out.

Ibrahim looked back.

"Can I write you?"

"Yes, you can," he said, walking away.

FORTY-FOUR

Under the shade of the tamarind tree in Amadu's Tillaberi compound, I sat at my loom and worked on an eight-inch-wide strip of blanket—a white background with black diamonds, green squares, and a red knot of wisdom at the strip's center. When finished, the strip would measure six feet in length. Although it had been years since I had woven, I hadn't forgotten what Amadu had taught me. Seated next to me, Seyni worked on a black, gold, and red Songhay wedding blanket. Several men from the neighborhood had placed themselves on palm-frond mats to watch us. A radio played scratchy lute music as a griot's voice recounted the courage of a soldier in the distant past.

A bank of fleecy white clouds had formed above the mesa east of Tillaberi. Periodic breezes from the west offered relief from the stifling heat of the Nigerien rainy season.

"Should we expect rain today?" I asked.

"With the breeze from the west," said one of the observers, an old man, short and thin, "we might get rain at dusk or in the evening."

"I hope so," Seyni said. "The millet has come up out of the sand in my fields. It needs a good rain. Let's hope it will come today or tomorrow."

"May God will it," another of the observers intoned.

I had been in Tillaberi for several days. I hadn't expected to spend much time there during this very short trip, and I certainly hadn't expected to weave again. And yet, after my meeting with Ibrahim, I grasped for the first time the true depth of Amadu's wisdom. Years before Amadu had somehow understood why it was important for me to weave. The old man went to great lengths to show me how to manipulate warp and weft. He introduced me to age-old designs, including the knot of wisdom, the knot that harmonizes the forces of the world. Human beings, Amadu had taught me, spend much of their time tearing the fabric of the world. "It's the burden of the weaver," he had said, "to create new fabrics, new blankets—to weave the world."

At the time I had considered Amadu's statement nothing more than a beautifully poetic metaphor. In the ensuing years, I had written extensively about Songhay weaving. Despite those years of study and reflection, I now realized that I had been blind to the central truth of weaving: one wove to remake a world that is continuously torn apart by jealousy, resentment, and bad faith. Woven threads reinforce the human spirit. They heal the wounds of the world. Like the blessed rains in the Sahel, they bring new life to parched fields.

Having met Ibrahim, I finally understood just how severely I had torn the fabric of the world. I would never be able to completely erase the scars left from the wounds I had opened along my path. In the ensuing years, I had tried to right many of my wrongs, but without resolution. I would never be entirely free of my past, but now I would try to live more in the present.

With that realization, I had set out for Tillaberi to weave. I knew that I had only one week—perhaps enough time to complete one strip of a blanket. I explained this decision to Elli. Although she wanted me to spend my last week in Niger with her, she encouraged me to go.

My trip to Tillaberi followed the customary pattern: haggling at the taxi depot, numerous stops along the road to discharge or pick up passengers, several flat tires, and tiresome police stops. At the sleepy Tillaberi depot, a solitary truck, empty of cargo, stood in the sunlight. Several men sat in the shade of the ticket office veranda. I looked for the prone figure of Angu, the educated dispatcher, asleep on a bench in the shade. I was saddened to learn that Angu, who suffered from liver disease, had died several years earlier. As in times past, I found some young boys to carry my bags. In the heat of midafternoon we made our way across the dunes to Amadu's compound.

The compound, which seemed unchanged, shimmered in the afternoon haze. At the compound entrance, I clapped three times and announced myself. Seyni, thick and solid and now the father of five children, walked to the entrance and smiled broadly.

"Welcome, David," he said extending his hand. Maymouna, his mother, and his two wives and children greeted me. The oldest boy, perhaps ten years old, took my bags and put them in his father's mud-brick house. "You've come to weave, haven't you?" Seyni asked.

"I need to weave one strip in one week."

"Well, you'd better get started. Your loom and stone are still here. Let's get you set up. There's much work to do."

"Thank you, brother," I said, realizing that my loom would always have its place in this compound. The next morning I started to weave. I had made much progress.

The bank of clouds on the eastern horizon thickened and darkened. Perhaps it would rain that day. The wind hadn't yet changed direction—a sure sign of an impending storm. On the radio, a monochord violin had replaced the lute. One of Seyni's wives brought a bowl of cool millet porridge and a bowl of water. Flies buzzed over the bowls.

"Do you think I'll finish this strip soon?" I asked Seyni.

"It looks like you'll finish it tomorrow, inshallah."

"May God will it," I said. "I want to give it to Elli."

"You've talked about her a great deal. She is your present and future, David. I've seen it in the shells."

"She is my present and my future," I repeated. Inspired by this new mantra, I worked my loom. The bank of clouds dissipated, leaving scattered bands of orange that streaked across the sky like so many bolts of cloth. As the sun slipped lower to the west, the bands of orange became broken strands of pink that then dissolved into a purple wave. Night consumed the last traces of light.

After a long, productive day, I would soon be asleep. Like the sun, I would rise the next day to finish the blanket and in my own small way remake the world.

NEW YORK 1998

Having told my story, I slumped in my seat. Like our guests, I had consumed three glasses of strong green tea, which provided a substantial jolt. Even so, I never liked to talk too much about my personal life—especially to strangers. But despite my emotional fatigue, the telling had elated me. Elli was right: it was psychologically liberating to tell my story to Africans—people who would more fully understand the dramas of my life. Mamadou and Daouda were a captive audience. Nevertheless, perhaps this telling would be the first step to writing a memoir.

Although darkness had long since settled on the streets of Soho, none of us in Gallery Bundu had looked at our watches.

Mamadou stood up and stretched. "Can we drink more tea?"

"There is always more tea," I said. "I'll prepare a new batch." I stood up to go to the kitchen.

"Sit down, David," Elli insisted. "I'll do it." She slipped off to the kitchen.

"So tell me, David," Mamadou wondered, "did you finish the blanket strip?"

"Yes, I did," I answered. "I finished it and gave it to Elli. I then left for New York. Elli came several weeks later. Ever since then, we've been together. The strip hangs in our apartment."

"And then?" Mamadou asked.

"I went back to teaching. Elli worked as a psychologist . . ."

"Part time," Elli added from the kitchen.

"That's right, part time. Then we pooled our resources to open Gallery Bundu."

Daouda said something to Mamadou in Sonnike, which Mamadou translated. "He wants to know if you ever hear from the people in Niger."

"I hear from Adam several times a year," I said, smiling. "He's become a famous soccer player in Niger. He's even been in World Cup competitions. I saw him last year when he played in France. His mother's restaurant is thriving in Niamey."

"Do you hear from Ibrahim?"

"I don't hear from him so much," I said, subdued. "He lives in France. Several years ago, he got his university degree."

"Has he become a professor?" Mamadou asked.

"Not yet. Last I heard, he was working in a bookstore and trying to write a book."

"Do you think you'll see him again?"

"I don't know."

"And what happened to Zeinabou?"

"Not a word."

"Did Diop ever make it to New York?"

Elli brought in the tea platter and sat down. "Yes, he did," she said. "He's come several times. On his first trip, he stayed for two months. After we took him around the city, he hooked up with a chauffeur and took his wood to Chicago, Minneapolis, and Detroit. He even went to Charleston, South Carolina, and Atlanta. Diop loves it here. He really likes Big Macs and Whoppers."

"He comes every year now, usually in the spring," I added. "We work well together—always have."

Mamadou picked up his glass of tea. He looked at Daouda, his compatriot, who spoke at length. Mamadou smiled. "My friend is from a family of storytellers. He liked your story, but is curious about its moral."

"I only wanted to talk about my experiences," I said.

"Yes," Mamadou nodded, "and you did a good job. But my friend says that your life teaches a lesson."

"Which is . . . ?" I asked, leaning toward him with curiosity.

"It's what Amadu told you when you were young and became his student. He told you that one always pays a price for power. He paid a price and so did you."

Hearing my own thoughts so clearly expressed by the young

African, I felt a burden lift off my shoulders. For years I had repressed the central truth of my life: that I had naively exchanged "a normal family life" for esoteric knowledge. This acknowledgment diminished the regrets I had harbored. I looked at Mamadou and took a deep breath of gratitude. "As always, Amadu was right," I acknowledged.

Mamadou leaned forward and spoke to me. "For an American, you're a pretty good storyteller." He paused and smiled at us. "Are you ready to hear a *really* interesting story?"

AUTHOR'S NOTE

Writing a book, no matter its form, is never a solitary enterprise. As always, I have many people to thank for their contributions. Carolyn Ellis read the manuscript of *Gallery Bundu* with great care, and her many constructive suggestions have improved the quality of the book. Jasmin Tahmaseb McConatha read every page with her characteristic thoroughness. Her comments have made this a more reader-friendly work. At the University of Chicago Press, T. David Brent steered the book through the evaluation and publication process with enthusiasm, energy, and economy—qualities that any author greatly appreciates. The skillful copyediting of Lois Crum tightened the narrative and polished the prose. Finally, I'd like to thank the dynamic and creative West African art traders whom I've come to know. Their economic agility and cultural sophistication have been inspiring.